Settling The Sangre's

PART 1
Out Of The Frying Pan
By D.C. Ludlow

Out Of The Frying Pan

Settling The Sangre's, Volume 1

D.C.Ludlow

Published by D.C.Ludlow, 2024.

OUT OF THE FRYING PAN

First edition. February 5, 2024.

Copyright © 2024 D.C.Ludlow.

ISBN: 979-8224406814

Written by D.C.Ludlow.

A story of adventure, pioneering, and westward expansion into the Rocky Mountains and a place many had started to simply call Colorado.

My name is Silas Horn.

I am a trapper, and one of the first to be known as a *free* trapper, in the wilds known as the Rocky Mountains. Now, I have been called a lot of things in my life; Officer in the United States Navy, pirate, criminal, and prisoner. Even my guide and friend, Long Walker, calls me Wandering Dog. I could never tell if it was an insult or a compliment, but that didn't matter to me anyway.

But I digress.

I guess there's some truth in all these things but first and foremost, I love to see new places. If I were to give weight to any words to describe myself I would use 'gentleman adventurer', but that may be a bit of a stretch. I have traveled to places no white man has seen before, despite the adherent risks.

I was always this way.

Never one to feel the need to remain at home, even as a child I would fritter away the hours finding new places to play ranger in the woods near my home. As I grew older, the need to find and see new places only grew into an overwhelming drive to GO! I have seen mountains no white man ever has before! I have been to places only Indians dared go!

But now as I grow older and wiser, I wish for a place to call *my own*. A home where I can live my life as I choose and not beholden to some king, president, or governor of any kind! This modern life has become twisted and overrun with new-fangled inventions and machines that are supposed to make life easier for humankind. But to me, the wild places have always drawn me to them! The deafening silence of the open plains, or the roar of a furious sea. If there was somewhere to go to see something new, I *went*!

Well, now, even some of the wild places have become filled with the King's men. The East India Trading Company and the Hudson Bay Company are growing rich from the work of men like me, while we remain poor. Well, that will simply not do for *me*! I will go further, I will go higher, and I will assume the risk of danger so that I may remain *free!*

Free trappers like me work for ourselves and we do it with a lust for adventure and the sheer will to survive even the harshest climates to do what we love! For some, it is about the money they can make from not having to use all their profits to resupply from the Company's stores. For others, it is an escape from a shady past. And for a few, it is an opportunity to turn one's life around and be someone new!

But for *me*, I love the adventure! What will I encounter around the next bend, or over the next ridge? Now that I have found these Rocky Mountains, I want to see them all! Maybe, just maybe, among my adventures there I will find a place that I can finally call *home!*

Chapter 1

As I topped a little rise in the landscape, to catch my breath and survey my surroundings a bit, I dropped to a crawl until I was flat on my belly at the top of the hill. It would not be prudent to show my shape against the open sky for all who may be near to see. That would be a dead giveaway of my location.

I knew my pursuers couldn't be more than half a day behind me, easily close enough to pick a man's shape out of the wilderness sky if they were looking in the right place at the right time. Looking to my rear and scanning the way I had come, I could see nothing of my enemy, but then again, I didn't expect to either. It had been two days since I had seen any sign of the Indians chasing me and, even at that, it was only a puff of dust on a hillside that gave them away. One of them probably slipped going down that steep grade *I* had gone around on my way through. That puff of dust was the only reason I knew the Indians had not given up the chase yet. But it also told me they were closing the distance behind me.

All I could do was keep going and get to safer country before they caught up with me and recaptured me. I had narrowly escaped death the first time, and I had no desire to be back in the hands of those who had nearly ended my life once already.

Turning my attention to the landscape in front of me, that I still needed to cross before I reached my companions and relative safety, I started to make mental notes of where I might find water and food. Preferably small game, as it had been more than three days since I had eaten a bite of anything. And at that, it was only a mouthful of venison jerky and some pemmican, both of which had run out days ago.

In front of me lay a low winding valley with scatterings of mountain pines and aspen groves in which deer and elk would be. Among the rolling hills between me and the tree line were bound to be more scattered antelope like I had seen several times on this trip but was not hopeful of getting close enough for a shot. Even if I *did* get that close, I was without powder and shot for my rifle anyway.

Off to my right, I could see a small band of elk grazing in the open. They were beautiful and graceful creatures to watch, and though I loved to watch them graze unaware, I knew I had to keep moving today. Beyond the elk, I could see the cedars and junipers and twisted mountain pines that gave me my next form of any cover for my movements. There might be turkeys or sage hens, probably in abundance, but too far out of my way to be of any use to me either.

Today, my way must be over the tall peaks in front of me that would put a wall between me and my enemies behind me. The way I had come was probably blocked with snows by now and I was going to have to find a different way to cross the masses of rock that blocked my way. I had come this way at the beginning of the season, in hopes of finding new and fresh streams of beaver to trap and possibly find amenable Indians, like the ones I had dealt with in the Northwest Territory who were open to trading with the whites. But now that seemed ages ago and I began to wonder as to the wisdom (or lack thereof) in this decision to explore further alone.

It was true I had taken many furs; beaver, fox, minks, weasels, and others, though it was chiefly the beaver fur I was in search of, for they gave the best price at rendezvous. I had hidden my bundles before the Indians caught up with me and now I was running for my life. But if I didn't live to collect the caches of furs I had been collecting for the last two months, all my efforts and risk would be in vain. My gamble to cross the mountains and delve into a new and unexplored territory would be for nothing. Even if I did live to tell about it; the telling of it would pay nothing.

No, I must survive this chase, cross the mountains, and find my partners, or I may as well just lay where I was and wait for the damned Indians to catch up to me and finish what they started when they captured me trespassing on their territory and taken me prisoner.

Taking a sip of the last of the little water I had, I looked once more over the way I had come. I assured myself I saw no sign of the small party of Indians who were after me, I turned once again to my flight.

Having noticed evidence of a small stream to the left of my position, I began my descent by crawling in that direction slowly, until I was far enough down the hill to be able to stand up from the tall grasses and walk without being seen from behind.

I felt grateful the winter had so far been somewhat dry in this region and I had not had to contend with much snow. Although I was still in the lower part of the mountains, what lay before me looked awful white indeed. My eyes kept finding themselves on the snow-capped peaks. I hoped my secret passage was clear still.

It was not long before I came upon the stream and found I was not the only creature in the area looking for water. I slowed my approach to a heel-to-toe creep, perfected by years spent hunting in the wilderness as a young man. Quietly, so as to not frighten away the small group of mule deer that had gathered at the stream to drink and graze the greens around it, I hoped to get close enough to injure one with a good throw with my camp ax. Slowly, I crept behind a stand of cedars with tumbleweeds stuck in it to take off my pack and free my limbs for a good strong throw. When I was out of sight of the beasts at the stream, I set my pack and possibles down silently, all the while keeping my eyes on the smallest, closest animal. I laid my rifle down and put the fingers of my right hand to my lips to breathe warmth onto them while I slowly drew my tomahawk from my belt with my left. I had hit many a target with a tomahawk, whether in sport or fights with the Indians in the past, quite accurately and skillfully, but never a deer and never when the need for an accurate throw was more great.

As I crept around the cedars to get a clear throw, the deer all suddenly bolted at top speed and disappeared into the scrub brush. Even as my disappointment overcame me at having lost the opportunity for fresh venison, I soon discovered the reason for the animals' flight.

In rounding the cedars I had frightened a large rabbit out from under one of the boughs of the cedars. The sudden movement had alerted the deer to my presence and spooked them off. A frightened deer, or group of deer especially, will run off sometimes several hundred yards before stopping to check their surroundings for any predators.

Not so with rabbits.

This particular rabbit had only scampered off about thirty feet or so and stopped just short of a thicket of junipers and brambles, counting on its stillness to keep it safe. Slowly, I turned away from the rabbit as if I hadn't seen it and stooped to pick up a rock. I had always been good at throwing stones when I was a boy and had brought many birds, squirrels, and other small game home to my mother's pot. Only now I had no pot, of course. As I stepped almost out of sight of the quivering rabbit I suddenly whipped the rock straight and hit the rabbit square in the head. This of course was not enough to kill the animal outright but gave me plenty of time to run up on it and wring its neck while it tried in vain to run away, not realizing it was on its side going nowhere.

Looking around me quickly and finding the day mostly done, I found suitable cover and decided to make camp in that spot for the night.

I retrieved my pack and rifle and took out my folding knife from the pocket on my pack. Taking my water skin and the rabbit down to the stream, I filled up my skin and proceeded to skin the rabbit and clean it in the cold water.

In this land, I felt as though I was a man in my natural environment. It took me mere seconds to remove the skin and guts of the rabbit and prepare it to cook; less time than it took most men to tie on their moccasins.

It wasn't long before I had gathered sticks and wood enough from around the bases of the trees to get a small fire going to cook the hare and warm my feet. Being mostly cedar wood, the fire had little smoke and I wasn't concerned with it giving away my position to my pursuers. The clump of cedars was not only good cover, but the thicket of shorter trees would also help filter out what little smoke the fire did make, and I felt confident my little camp was secure for the night.

While the rabbit roasted over the tiny fire, I gathered up more wood I might need during the night and prepared for the first sleep I had had in three days. I knew at this point I would be in no more danger when I awakened than I was now, and anyway, I was tired and needed sleep if I was going to continue.

I kept my fire low, barely a flame to be seen for more than a few feet from my spot under the trees, but just large enough to cook my meal and warm my limbs from the chill evening air.

If anyone was there to see, I might be mistaken for one of the savages that tracked me. I was dressed in a hunting shirt and leggings of fringed buckskin which had been tanned and smoked to a rich golden brown, and moccasins made from the tough hide of a buffalo that wrapped around my legs up to my knees, secured there with laces cut from rawhide. My coat was made of buffalo with the hair still on for insulation against the cold mountain air where I spent my winters trapping beaver in these rocky mountains. Atop my head, I wore a cap of beaver fur with a small brim made from beaver tail to shade my eyes. Secured to the side of the hat with a brass medallion was an eagle feather that I was given by a member of a friendly tribe in the Northwest Territories. In my experience a beaver hat was warmer than the woolen caps the Frenchmen seemed to favor.

My face and hands were tanned as brown as the buffalo moccasins I wore, from years spent out in the open in the sun and wind, and scarred from many battles with Mother Nature and her native children, the Indians of the mountains where I carried out the tasks of my chosen profession.

I was a trapper. And one of the first to be known as free trappers. Free trappers didn't work for any company, we didn't conform to the crown, we worked for ourselves and did a dangerous job not many could do, and we did it well.

I was not a Company Man, as many were in those days, but was a member of a small party of other free trappers and privateers in the fur trade industry made up of several men from the American states, as well as a few Canadians and members of the so-called 'civilized tribes' from east of the Missouri River. What set me apart from others in my party, other than the fact I stood well over six feet tall and wore a buffalo coat, was the length of the rifle I chose to carry.

Most trappers (and more fortunate Indians of that day) chose to carry a Hawken rifle, a good hunting rifle proven for its ease to carry afoot or on horseback. Instead, I chose to carry a modified "Kentucky" long rifle that had belonged to my father. The modification being the replacement of the flintlock with the more modern cap-lock firing system, and the addition of a more modern sight being used on the more expensive hunting rifles sold back east for sport hunters.

The cost of these modifications was so much that I went somewhat meagerly supplied the year I had them done that season. But the lack of sugar and flour and other camp luxuries was well replaced with the abundance of fresh game I could bring down with it at a longer distance than any of my contemporaries. Not to mention the added furs such as fox, coyote, mountain lions, and bear to be sold at rendezvous as well. That had been a tough season without coffee or corn meal, and half of it with no salt for the meat I could shoot, but it had proven well worth the investment in the long run. The profits from the extra furs allowed me to outfit a party of men myself the next season. Not only this, but to outfit them in such a way as to be the envy of many others that year.

That was last year. Through my ideas and practices, as well as my somewhat spartan outfitting, I was able to make another good season and paid my debts with the traders, and have enough to bring these men together again for another season. And have leftovers. I figured I only broke even, having supplied ten men and myself with nearly half the supplies needed to sustain such a party through a harsh winter trapping season.

My men, having reaped the lion's share of the profits from last season, this year had supplied themselves with winter clothing, food, weapons, and other such possibles but trusted me with the procurement of powder, shot, traps, and other gear, as I had the year before. I had convinced them of the value of my ideas on how to run and supply a successful and profitable trapping season. As a result, they had *all* profited more than any other year before, and in truth, more than any other privately funded party in the Rockies that year.

Now, as I picked every last morsel of meat from the bones of the roasted hare, I wondered if perhaps I had cast my lot on too thin a premise; too much inhospitable territory. I wondered if my grand ideas would be the death of me, if I would ever return to my party with the richness in furs I had prophesied. Or would I leave my bones to bleach in the sun, never to be heard from again. Many a man had gone adventuring and never . . .

"ENOUGH! Nary a negative thought has produced a positive outcome!" I said quietly aloud.

From my pack, I produced a tin cup and filled it with water from my skin canteen, and set it on a flat rock that I had placed over the fire. As the water warmed, I got out my tea box. A little wooden box carved with a flowery design that contained crushed herbs and flowers of my own gathering. I sprinkled a little of the mixture into the cup and inspected the remainder in the box and added a little more. *Waste not want not*, I thought. *But what the hell, nothing lasts forever.*

When the tea had brewed to a sufficient pinkish color I took the cup from the coals. I was just about to add more fuel to my little fire, as the night was starting to cool significantly, when I heard a sound some distance away.

There are many rustlings and scratchings to be heard at night in the wilderness and, my ear being tuned to them all, there was something about this particular sound that didn't fit into the night air as a natural sound should. I loosened my blade in its sheath and then sat motionless for many minutes straining my ears for more of this sound so I could try to identify it, but didn't hear it again.

I decided perhaps it would be better if I kept the fire to a minimum for the time being and picked up my cup to drink its contents before it got cold. Half of the medicine's worth was in the warmth when it was consumed. I added only the smallest twigs to the fire in order to feed the coals and still keep the light low.

When I finished the tea I carefully set it aside. I focused my ears on the sounds of the night, and my eyes on the white capped mountain range in front of me in the moonlight. I let my mind drift where it will until sleep came to overtake me. Though I did not chance to lay down to sleep, I pulled my buffalo coat tighter around me and leaned back into a notch between the two trees under which I sat. I didn't know when my lids finally closed and sleep overtook me, but behind my closed lids, as I slept I dreamed again of the same woman I had seen in I dreams for quite some time now. Always the same woman, the same smile, and always the same sense that I must find her and save her. . . From what I had no idea and the dream never foretold; just that I owed her and I must rescue her from . . . .

When I opened my eyes again, it was still dark. It was my habit to wake and begin the day before dawn. My fire had long since gone cold so I covered it with a dead branch and gathered my belongings. After dusting my little campsite with pine needles and stray branches to cover my presence, I shouldered my pack with a grunt, picked up my rifle, and set my sights on the mountains in front of me. I had been using a set of twin peaks as my bearings for the way I needed to go but this morning there was a thick fog covering the valley. I knew which direction to go and could figure out the exact way once the sun came and burned off the fog.

With a sigh of determination, I began to walk. I had always hated the fog. It seemed unnatural things happened within it. It was certainly harder to keep watch on one's back trail and was very easy to get lost in a thick fog if one was not familiar with the terrain. And right now, even though I had come this way, I was definitely *not* familiar with the terrain.

By the time the sun broke over the hills behind me I was about five or six miles from where I had spent the night. I knew that by taking the few hours rest I risked letting my pursuers catch up to me, but if I hadn't they would have had a better chance of running me down anyway. I kept checking my back trail but with the fog it was hard to make anything out. In the back of my thoughts I wondered if perhaps they had given up but better reasoning told me *No they're comin..* and there were three of them.

It was at that moment I decided to change the game. I was tired of being chased and hunted and it was time to change the rules. What better way to not get caught but to turn the tables and hunt the ones hunting me. After all this may be their game but this was my *LIFE* and I was a fast learner. I took a sip or two from my water skin and began to take stock of my current situation through different eyes.

Turning my back to the mountains, I stood for a long while, motionless, surveying the land for any signs of movement. A rabbit a few yards away, a flight of birds overhead, a few hundred yards off a few dots that could only be antelope, picking the grass through the sparse snow on the ground. As I thought, I looked over the terrain.

First off, I had no powder and no shot for my rifle; at the moment it was dead weight. To stand and fight or kill three men I needed ammunition for my rifle, but not for one man. I also had knife and tomahawk. So; what I needed to do was separate one from the other two. I began to search the area for the right ground to use to fight this battle. I began to formulate a plan in my mind. . . but how would I draw them near enough without giving myself away. . without suspecting my trap?

Chapter 2

On the other side of the mountains, Tom Sweet was halfway through checking his traps for the day. So far it had been an average day with less-than-average results. He had only pulled three beavers, six weasels, and a fox today. He didn't count the coyote; he guessed the wolves had gotten to it first. He had seen tracks of wolves around the area but around the trap itself was only the confused jumble of tracks left by rats, wild cats, and other small vermin, a few bones and tufts of fur useless to a trapper.

He did keep the head, though.

His companions all thought he was out of his bean for collecting skulls as well as furs but he didn't care; he had his own ideas of which they knew nothing. That was the way he liked it.

A large man, though not a tall one, Tom was as strong and hardy an Irishman as there ever was. Standing about eight inches over five feet tall, he wasn't much of an imposing figure until one assessed the whole man at once. He was probably 200 pounds of solid, corded muscle from long years of hard work, whether in the service of the Army as a young man, or from the hard labor as a farmer before that. Maybe it was the years spent as a blacksmith in Georgia after the army or the work it was to climb mountains and trek through beaver ponds frozen in ice.

Wide at the shoulders and narrow-hipped, he was a formidable man to face when angered. Though he was of good temper, many had crossed him and wished they hadn't. In those days, he always dressed in buckskin pants fringed down the leg and tucked into tall moccasins lined with parts of an old wool blanket too worn to be of use any longer. His shirt of calico was worn over woolen long johns and tied at the waist with a green sash, behind which he kept his knife and a pistol. Over the rest, he wore a red capote made from a trade blanket he'd bought at rendezvous.

He wore a coyote fur hat on his head to cover the hair he was missing. He liked the fact it made him feel he could blend into the background and be mistaken for just another coyote if someone looking wasn't paying too much attention. It was useful for hunting as well. Deer, elk and buffalo all knew what a man looked like. They feared him and would run as they had been hunted by the natives for centuries. But they also knew that a coyote alone was no threat, so if they saw Tom creeping up on them for a hunt, they would stand until he was nearly among them, not even realizing he was about to shoot one of them. He was pretty good at it too and sometimes would sneak up on elk or moose, for no other reason than to impress his compatriots.

Tom was not exactly a good-looking man with the way the years had been hard on him. Leathery face and hands, a broad nose flattened in a fight once or twice, and hair that was thin on top. What flowed from under his hat was wild and matted, as he didn't take much care of it until it started to knot up. He'd just cut it off with his knife.

"I never been a pretty man and I never will be," he'd say. "So, what do I care what I look like . . . I don't have to look at me!"

He was from New York originally, and being the only 'Nor' Easter' in the crew, he kept pretty much to himself. Tom and I had met three years earlier, partially by accident, at a rendezvous in the northern territory on the banks of the big river they called the Columbia River. It had another name but since no white man could pronounce it, it was simply named for Columbus.

Tom knew these mountains like the back of his hand now that he had been here for three years straight. Tom was perfectly happy to be in the mountains, far away from people.

Tom was my right-hand man. He was my friend and business partner, but more than that, he called himself my brother. We had fought together in many battles with Indians, or with men of lesser character who liked to trade in other's furs at rendezvous. In fact, in one of these skirmishes, he saved my life. I knew then he and I were to be good partners in these wild lands. And great friends.

It was the year I had my rifle, 'Long Stick' as it became to be known, modified for cap and ball, we had met. Tom had had a particularly bad run of luck that year and decided to sell his traps and quit. He and I met while I was looking to buy some. One of the other trappers had heard I was looking to supply a small crew for the winter and told him to find me to sell his traps.

Like many trappers that year, I didn't have the money for more equipment because of spending it on converting my rifle to a more modern and reliable firing system. Although, I did invite the stocky little Irishman to have a meal and a drink with me instead. Tom agreed.

"What kind of Irishman would I be if I refused a drink?" he'd said.

By the next morning, we both had serious hangovers from the cheap whiskey sold at the rendezvous, but after a night of drunken revelry, tall tales, and comparing scars, I made the leap to offering Tom a partnership. Once I had laid out my plans for the season Tom skeptically agreed, lured by the generous offer to resupply him with powder, shot, flour, salt, sugar, coffee, and a whole list of other supplies more than enough to live and work all season. The catch was that there would be two of us living off those supplies, not just one. He balked a little at this, but eventually believed my promise to provide the rest with Long Stick. The kicker was that we wouldn't have regular wall tents or any real shelter like most company men used.

"Them tents are heavy, Tom, and we will be in hostile country," I had told him. "It will be better if we don't have a heavy tent to have to move around all the time." Instead, we would use a smaller and more versatile kind of system that I had thought up.

"It musta been the whiskey," Tom would later tell people, but he agreed. We would need fewer horses and no mules. And if I was right about the furs we could gather, who but a dullard would *not* agree?

As it went in those days, there were many tall tales and stories. Mountains of gold where you can pick up a fortune in a day, stories of giant men and great hairy elephants with tusks longer than a man is tall, or the infamous legend of Cortez and his gold stolen from the Aztecs. But a secret valley full of fat beaver ripe for the taking was one familiar to Tom, as he had heard it again and again in his time with the Company.

"But I *found it*!" I told him. "A hidden valley! Rich with furs and virtually open for the taking, as the Indians don't go there much in the winter."

"If *this* tall tale *is* true," Tom had remarked. "There is no doubt we shall succeed!" He was certainly astounded when I took him and showed him the spot.

It had been right under his nose for two years, and Tom had not even thought to look in the place where it was. Hidden behind a peak everyone just assumed was *just* a mountain peak . . . but in reality, was a long thin valley nearly five miles long by a mile wide hidden behind the mountain.

There were numerous beaver damns and ponds, as well as all kinds of other game naturally concentrated by the geology of the valley. It was also a beautiful place during the right time of year. Pinyon pines and tall twisted cedars, juniper bushes, scrub oaks, and sagebrush. In the summer, wildflowers by the thousands grew wherever the eye could see, and streams of clean, pure water ran through the valley, keeping everything green and new.

In the winter it was a harsh landscape of snow and ice, with windswept valley floors and drifts of snow in the hills and woods taller than a man stands by far. And it was winter when the fur business was at its peak. The work involved was backbreaking and dangerous, not only because of the environment but because of the Indians as well. Many of the tribes did not like white men delving so deep into their sacred territories and hunting grounds. Some tribes had been in these mountains since the beginning of time, and they fought bloody hard to protect them.

Despite all the dangers, me and Tom did well that season. In fact, we had the best season in almost a decade since we both began trapping after the war. When I divvied up the profits and Tom saw the advantages of working with me, our partnership, if not secure before, was cemented then. This was also the reason the next season we were able to outfit ten men my way!

If I had told Tom, "Next season, we trap the valleys of the moon."

Tom would have had only one question, "How we gonna git there?"

Now, as he stood up and stretched his back after pulling a big beaver out of the ice, Tom was worried. He told me at camp one night he had thought to himself in that moment *What has become of Silas? He should have been back by now from wherever he has gone. I wish Silas was not so secretive.* But he understood why I was. He knew it was a good thing in the long run that I was, but Tom was still worried.

Chapter 3

Black Coyote motioned to his two fellow warriors that he heard something and to stop moving. Dull Knife and Running Elk both strained their ears but heard only their own breath and their hearts beating. They didn't doubt that Black Coyote had heard something and were waiting to hear it themselves. Black Coyote just grunted and pointed in the direction he had heard the sound come from and began to creep slowly in that direction. He motioned for the other two to fan out on either side of him and search the ground for a sign. This white man was as good at covering his tracks as any he had ever tracked before. Maybe better.

But Dull Knife, Running Elk, and himself were the best trackers in the village, which was why they were selected to hunt down the white man when he escaped. This one proved to be wily as well, for he had fooled Young Bear and Grey Eagle so well he had not only been able to escape them but was able to escape with his weapons as well as his life! This infuriated Black Coyote as the long rifle the man carried was to be *his* trophy for capturing the trespassing white man.

The three had not gone more than a couple hundred yards when they all stopped in their tracks. They had *all* heard it that time! The sound of a mouse when it's in pain and dying. The high-pitched squealing was unmistakable.

But something was off.

There should have been the sounds of its predator as well . . . but there were none. Not only that but if it *was* some predator killing a mouse, there would not be the *continued* squealing! All three drew the same conclusion at once without one word between them.

Black Coyote motioned to his fellow warriors to circle to the right and the left of his position as they moved forward. Now they all knew their prey had set a trap and was waiting for them to rush in force to attack and kill him, so splitting up and flanking him was the best way to go.

Black Coyote took an arrow from his bearskin quiver and nocked it to his short bow as he slowly moved forward, silently stalking this trespasser. He had not gone more than a dozen steps when he heard a startled shout from Dull Knife on his right, then the sound of a brief struggle . . . and silence. To his left, he heard a songbird twitter; a signal from Running Elk that he was coming back to meet him. He too had heard the same sounds.

If Dull Knife had met the white man and fought him and won, they would have heard him *whoop* as he attacked and his victorious, "AI! AI! AI! AI!" as he stood over him with the man's scalp. But there was no sound and they knew Dull Knife was dead. They quickly decided to go investigate. Perhaps they would come across the white as he stripped Dull Knife's body of any useful weapons.

They were not so lucky.

When they arrived at the place where Dull Knife had taken his last breath, they found his body hanging upside down swinging from a rope by one leg from a branch of a tall pine. They also found he was stabbed in the heart and had had his throat cut from ear to ear, his blood streaming down and dripping into a pool on the ground. The wound in his neck was so severe it had nearly severed his head completely. They both stood for a moment as their friend bled his life into the ground and said their death blessings for his spirit before they turned their attention back to their prey.

Now there were tracks to follow, as the man had hurried when he left Dull Knife's body to swing in the breeze. Confident that they would soon catch and kill this trespassing white man, they quickly followed the tracks deeper into a thicket of junipers, young spruce, and twisted cedars, arrows at the ready on their bow stings and eyes keen in the shadows of the forest searching for the white.

Soon the tracks they followed just stopped. It was like their prey had suddenly risen on wings and flown away to escape them. They quickly looked around for more signs but found none. There was simply no sign after his last step. They began a methodical search of the area by walking in wider and wider circles around the last clear track to see if there was any sign they could use to decipher where the man had gone. It was as if he had just vanished!

As they came back together to discuss their next move, Black Coyote heard a rush of air behind him and dropped to one knee just as Dull Knife's tomahawk buried itself in Running Elk's neck. He made no sound but stood there for a moment with a stunned look on his face, before dropping to his knees and then slumping to the ground dead at Black Coyote's feet.

The remaining warrior took no time to wish his friend's spirit well. There wasn't time for that now. There was not even time to wipe his friend's blood from his face. He rolled quickly into the brush at the side of the trail and carefully surveyed his surroundings. Making no sound other than the breath in and out of his mouth, he stayed crouched there for quite some time listening and watching. He heard and saw nothing to tell him where this white had gone! After about an hour he decided the white had escaped, and stood from his concealment to care for the bodies of his friends.

Perhaps his father had been right when he suggested taking more warriors with him to track this white man. But how could he have known this one white would be so hard to kill? Most were much easier!

I stayed motionless and quiet in my hiding spot, watching the Indian to see what he would do. It was apparent that he thought I had gotten away or he wouldn't reveal himself. Having lost his two friends, it was a toss-up whether he would continue the hunt or give up the trail and go back to his people to deliver the news and regroup. Either way, for now, I would remain hidden. I didn't like killing but it was necessary at times to survive.

I watched him remove the tomahawk from his friend's body and cut the other down from where he was still swinging by one leg. He then laid them out under a nearby tree and covered them with stones. I couldn't understand the words he said while he sprinkled earth in the air over their graves. I watched all this in silence and dared not move as I was aware of the tricky nature of Indians. I watched as he gathered up weapons and personal items to take back to the relatives. I watched as he looked around and turned to the east and began walking back toward the village. Yet I remained still long after the Indian was out of sight.

From where I was hiding (after quickly covering my tracks), I could see for quite some distance in all directions. I sat and watched as the Indian came back into view a few hundred yards down the trail as he stopped to adjust something he was carrying. When he began to walk again, I let a quiet sigh of relief watching him finally round a copse of cedars and spruce and disappear.

Only then did I stretch my legs a bit, but stayed in my perch. There were still a couple of hours of daylight left according to the sun and I needed the rest as well as to eat. Last night's rabbit would not carry me for long and now that I had taken a parfleche of pemmican and jerked meat from Dull Knife, I was content to sit and watch the sunset behind the mountain, watch the terrain, think about my new situation, and eat.

Chapter 4

The day waned into the evening as two men trudged wearily back to their camp carrying their catch for the day. Both were of average height and build with bright red hair and ruddy speckled complexion. They were both dressed in dirty buckskins and coats made of woolen blankets. Even a blind man could see they were brothers.

"Quite a good day's catch I'd say, don'tcha think?" said the taller and older of the two.

"If you say so, brudder," retorted the other. "Personally, I'm getting sick of this work."

"You never did like to do yer share, even as a kid. I *always* had to make excuses fer ya. But yer learnin' boy-o. Yer getting to be pretty good at this trappin' business, I must say. Now, ya just gotta learn how to skin 'em without butchering the fur. I know it's foreign to ya, Christopher me boy, but it's the *skins* we want here, lad. That's what buys the whiskey at rendezvous!"

"Awe, git off me back, David! Ye know I was never good at skinnin' beasties! *But*, give me one o' these savages and I'll have *his* hair in a second! Don't forget, brudder, where I came here from *that's* where the money is!" Chris almost shouted at his brother.

"Aye, and it almost kilt ye din't it, if'n I remember it correctly! And if'n I remember it in *full*, it were me who saved ya!! *In fact*, if it weren't fer me—"

Chris cut his brother off, "—Ya, ya, ya, ya, I know. I dun heard it a thousand times! Trying to scalp one before they're *all* dead don't pay, ya, ya, ya. And if *you* hadn't come and put a ball in the eye of the one savage I din't see, I'd be pushin' up daisies! I KNOW, I KNOW!"

"All righty then, boy-o," replied David, "And don'tcha fergit it, either!!"

"Ah, how can I, now? Ye remind me every other day! Jus' shut yer trap and show me what ya do wit' these little fellers here," Chris mumbled holding up a mink by one hind foot.

"It's jus' like skinnin' a rabbit, lad. Here, I'll show ye *one* more time and then yer on yer own!" grumbled David. "I'm tired of doin' yer work for ya, ya gotta start doin' it *all* fer yerself!"

"Why should I?" Chris retorted, barely able to hide his mirth. "When I can git me older, *more gullible* brudder to do it for me??" He slapped David in the back of the head with the little critter.

"OH! More of yer jokes it is, I see! Keep it up, brudder, and I'll git ye one of these days!" David spat and tossed the little creature back into his brother's lap. "Do it yerself, smart-arse! And do it *right* this time!" he blurted in an angry tone, all the while grinning like a cat and winking at his brother.

As they went to work skinning the day's catch, they both heard a twig snap in the distance.

"HSSSST!" came from David as a warning to his brother but Chris had already grabbed his rifle and disappeared. He heard the click of Chris'sHawkenrifle from behind a bush to his left and pretended he heard nothing else and went back to skinning the beaver at his feet.

Soon a voice came from the woods, "HALLOO! The camp! Is there a *sober* Irishman about?"

"Come and see fer yerself, stranger!" beckoned David. "But beware, a drunken Irishman can shoot jus' as well as a sober Scot, don'tcha know!"

"I'd have to see that to believe it!" came the reply.

"Ya, ya, ya, Samuel, ya old Scottish fart! Jus' come in and sit before ya fall down and I hafta pick ya up and carry ya!" Shouted David.

"Not until I see that murderin' brudder of yours put his rifle down," Samuel chuckled. "He might hurt himself wid it! Or shoot me by some accident!"

"Just like a MacGregor," laughed Christopher as he stood from his bush and uncocked his rifle. "To insult the man holdin' yer life by a trigger finger!"

Samuel MacGregor just laughed and walked into camp and set his rifle against a tree. "I see mountaineering is startin' to agree wit' you two," observed the Scot. "But a real mountain man woulda smelled me comin' and tossed some beaver tail on the fire for impending guests by now!"

With a quick jerk on the animal he was skinning, David cut off the tail and tossed it into the cold dead ashes of the long-dead fire. "Are ye happy now, Da?" he quipped.

"That's better boy, now., where's yer jug?" Samuel ignored the jibe.

"Only a swallow or two left in it but it's yonder in the crick there," Chris replied, then smiled. "But you'll be keepin' yer hands off'n it till the work's done and our bellies full and happy from supper first!" he added.

"I taught him that I did," said David with a wink. "Else there'd be no whiskey left and I'll have done all the work, while *he* does naught but drink all night and sleep all day, dreamin' of robbin' folks on the roads and killin' redskins!"

Chris spat into the ashes in the fire pit "Its a heap of a sight better than all this *WORK* out here in the wilds of ... oh thats right NOWHERE!" cried Chris as he began to put sticks together to start a fire. He took the beaver tail out of the ashes and tossed it to Samuel. "Heres yours ya bloody Scot, it ought to be about done enuff fer yas by now!

David cut and peeled a green alder stick while Samuel loaded his pipe. About the time Chris had a small blaze going David looked up from his work, "SO... what brings ya to grace OUR camp this evenin Yer Majesty?" "In a bit lad, best have a bite and a dram in yer belly afore we talk about this business. And a pipe to go with it as well, yer not gonna like this news" Samuel said gravely. Without taking his eyes off the Scotsman's face David said "Better go pull that jug from the crick Chris me lad.. I don't like the sound of this."

Chris looked up from skewering the beaver carcass to put over the fire which was crackling brightly by now. "Nor I," He said "Nor the look on Sam's face". As he went to the stream for the jug of whiskey he asked over his shoulder "Whats this news yer tryin *NOT* to tell us? Who died?" He pulled the jug from the stream and uncorked it and handed it to Samuel first as he was a guest with news. Samuel didn't answer right away but took a good long drink from the jug before handing it back. He wiped the rivulets of the firewater from his chin with his sleep and looked at David. "Here gimme a branch of that fire so's I can light me pipe before I break the news."

Chris handed the jug to David and took a stick from the fire to hand Sam before digging out his own pipe and tobacco, little of it as there was left. As David took a pull from the jug, Samuel finally spoke while lighting his pipe "I got the word from the headhunter today, Silas is two weeks overdue, and ye both know what that means!"

Chris froze with his pipe halfway to his mouth and holding a stick with an ember on it to light it and looked from Sam, to David, back to Sam, and exclaimed "Well I don't know what it means!! TELL ME!"

David handed Samuel the whiskey jug and said, "It *means,* me boy, that he may be done fer! We all knew it was a gamble, him goin' off by himself to Lord knows where on some whim!"

Sam took a short drink of the whiskey and set it down where any one of them could reach it.

Chris blurted, "So, what does that mean for us? I don't mean to be insensitive but ya know, really! He's a grown man! He knew the risks of comin' out here to this God-forsaken land for these rat beasties!" He leaned forward and took a stick from the fire to light his pipe.

"It means, me boy, that we all reap less fer our toils at rendezvous! Silas is a cagey one and, if you remember, he's the one with the contact within the Company that will pay the same for our beaver as they pay the Company men. If Silas don't come back, that means we're all on our own to negotiate with the buyers and traders . . . and you also know that the traders don't deal with the privateers until *after* They buy from the Company men," Samuel said.

For a moment there was only the sound of the fire crackling and fat sizzling that dripped off the beaver slowly roasting over the fire. Chris smoked his pipe while David took a long drink from the jug. Samuel tapped his pipe out on a tree root and watched the faces of his cousins. David was mulling over this morsel of information like a dog worrying a bone for the last bit of flavor hidden in the marrow, while Chris looked a little confused still.

Slowly, the younger of the McNeil brothers raised a finger in the air and let out a breath of smoke, and slowly asked, "Wait now, aren't most of the traders employed by the Company?"

"*Now* yer learning me boy!" replied Samuel. "And Silas used to be as well! That's how he gets the Company price for our furs!"

"But no one knows which trader Silas deals with, not even Tom!" David added.

"What about the Frenchies? They used to be Company men as well, din't they?" Chris asked.

"Yes, but that was up in the Northwest Territories not here in the Rockies!" David told him dryly. Again there was a pause in the conversation. This time, David broke the silence by handing the whiskey to Samuel and asking, "So, what's to be done, then?"

Samuel just smiled and answered "What's to be done, is ya turn that meat on the fire afore it burns to a crisp on one side and still raw on the other! No one likes a burnt beaver!"

Chris jumped up like he'd been stung by a wasp to turn the spit. It was nowhere near burning yet but cooking nicely. He turned the spit halfway to roast the other side of the beaver and tended to the coals, adding wood and rearranging the coals under the beaver better. "Are we gonna go lookin' fer him?" he asked.

"No one but he and God Almighty knows where he's gone!" replied Samuel. "And the Good Lord ain't answerin' . . . I asked already!"

After another short pause, David spat suddenly, "DAMN Silas for a tight-lipped fool! If not already so it'll be the death of him. Maybe US TOO!"

"Let's hope not," Samuel shot back. "Here, have another drink of this rotgut. Yer brother's bound and determined to starve me afore supper's cooked enough to eat it!"

The Brothers McNeil took that as a hint that the business talk was done for now.

"Aye, he's slow as a dead turtle at most things he is! But you wait, when you taste what he does with that beaver meat you'll think you've died and gone to Buckingham Palace!" Chris bragged. "Me brudder's a natural whiz with herbs and such! 'Tis a pity he's a drunkard only fit for cooking fer the likes of us here!"

David only replied by flipping a coal out of the fire into his brother's lap and laughing, as Chris began to dance a jig as good as any danced to a tune in a tavern to get rid of the fire branding him through his buckskins. Samuel just laughed and poked more tobacco into his pipe. This was one of the reasons he partnered with his two Irish cousins for this adventure.

. If nothing else, they were entertaining!

Chapter 5

Tom was just finishing up pressing and packing a bundle of furs to cache, when Long Walker, his friend and guide, strode up to the camp as silently as ever. It almost startled Tom but he was getting used to it.

"I've told you, Long, make some *noise* when ya come up behind me!" Long Walker just smiled as Tom went on. "Kick a stone or whistle like a whippoorwill or something, so's I know it's you and I don't shoot ya for a hostile!"

"I did," replied Long. "I made the sound of a cricket, you did not hear?"

"No! I did not!" retorted Tom dryly with a slight smile. "Next time, just shout like a white man . . . ya know . . . 'halooo the camp', so's I can hear ya! One of these days, someone's gonna shoot ya, thinkin' yer the enemy!" Tom pointed out. "Now, tell me what have you found about Silas?"

The scout put his musket butt on the toe of his moccasin and leaned on the barrel. Long Walker was an impressively tall and large man for an Indian. He was a member of the Ute tribe but had been exiled from his people. He was dressed like most of the mountain men he now worked and lived with. He wore tattered, ragged buckskins, dirty from travel and work. He carried an English musket he had taken as a war prize in a battle long ago in his youth, along with his crooked and bladed war club. He was probably older than he looked as he was, being smooth of skin and complexion. He wore his coal black hair in a long braid down his back and kept two eagle feathers tied into it. The only things that gave away his age were his eyes. They were dark and piercing, yet wise and knowing as well. There was a darkness in him that lay deep under the surface, but if one were to look into his eyes for any amount of time they would see he was, in fact, *much* older than he looked. He had been hired as a hunter and guide on this trip through this western territory; his tribe had been here for hundreds of years and considered themselves a part of the land. He had proven again and again he was worth his salt.

"I found tracks leading to the secret place you trap, and they lead into the valley and disappear near a lake at the top of the valley. No tracks lead out of that valley but I found no other sign," Long reported.

"Hmmm. It's mostly all rocky terrain up there," mused Tom almost to himself. "I wonder if he somehow . . ." Tom cut himself short, almost in disbelief of what he was thinking.

Those cliffs were 1000 feet high in some places, high above the lake, and capped with snow and ice this time of year. There was no way Silas had climbed those cliff walls to get to the other side. There had to be some other explanation!

He looked at Long Walker and said, "I believe we will go and lay some traps in that valley ourselves, Long. It's still rich with fur critters and now we have a mystery to solve!"

"It is good idea," Long replied. "When we go?"

"Two days," Tom replied. "It will take that long to gather the traps and cache the furs for when we get back. Did you look into that cave I told you about?"

The scout nodded and replied, "Is no bear cave. Good cache place for supply and furs if it is needed. No tracks."

"GOOD!" Tom exclaimed. "Get yourself something to eat and some coffee, you have horses to gather!"

The Ute answered with just one word, "Good," and sat by the fire and cut a strip of the venison roasting there then poured some coffee into a tin cup.

"And go easy on that sugar this time! That's the last we got till spring!" Tom shot back over his shoulder with a smile. Long Walker, like many of his kind, was a bit of a sugar addict, especially when it came to coffee. *How is it that someone who has gone their whole life without sugar could become such an addict in just a few short months is beyond me,* Tom thought to himself. *Mus' be tryin' to make up for lost time!*

"Coffee much better with more sugar," was the reply from the Ute. "Especially your coffee!" he added with a hint of a smile in his eyes.

"Oh, so *now* you insult my coffee too!" Tom countered. "Next you'll say ya don't like my cooking either!"

Long had just taken a bite of one of Tom's prized sourdough biscuits and he only smiled and replied through a mouth full of biscuit, "Biscuit dry!"

"Fine, you cook your own next time!" Tom rebutted.

The Ute just chuckled and kept eating.

Tom sat on a log across the fire from his friend, took a knife from his belt and cut a chunk of venison roast from the spit for himself, and put it in a biscuit cut in half. "What do *you* think Long? Do you think Silas could have climbed out of that valley to cross the peaks?"

The Ute merely shrugged in response and shoved half a biscuit in his mouth, adding to the meat he was already chewing. After he swallowed, he said, "Maybe Mr. Horn know how to fly," and took another bite of the venison.

Tom almost choked on a sip of his coffee. "Wouldn't surprise me in the least, my friend. Not in the least. Silas is a surprising man." The two men fell silent after that . . . as each knew that there was no more to say for the moment.

Chapter 6

When it finally grew dark and I had still seen no sign of the Indian's return, I figured it was safe to climb down from my perch high up in a twisted cedar tree. In fact the same tree as I had used to snare and kill Dull Knife.

As the other two had been saying their death blessing for their friend I had hidden among the branches and remained still. The spot I had chosen to ambush the natives was a thick grove of cedars, junipers, and pines, thick, tall, and close together.

When one of the Indians had their back to me, I risked a throw of the tomahawk giving away my position if I missed but was lucky it had hit its target, with surprising effect for such a light weapon. All I needed to do then was remain still and quiet in my perch, wait for the Indian to make up his mind what to do, and hope he didn't think to look up. Yes, it was a risk, but then again all my life had been one risk after another. My gamble had paid off; I was alive and my last pursuer had left, homeward bound, leaving me free to be on my way in relative safety.

My journey still would be by no means easy. It was a two-day walk just to the foot of the mountain I needed to climb to get back to my secret passage to the west face of the range. And as luck would have it, it was beginning to snow. The Indian had been nice enough to leave my rope in a heap at the base of the tree, so I retrieved that and coiled it up, then hung it in its place on my pack.

"I may need you yet," I said aloud, then chuckled at myself for talking to a rope.

I then went to the tree under which the bodies of my former enemies lay to pay my respects to fellow warriors fallen in battle, and to forgive them for trying to hunt and kill me.

War and fighting had been a part of most of my life and I had learned not to hate the men I fought. Instead, I admired them, these savages, these people on whose land I was the intruder. Another man may have taken their scalps to traders who dealt in the buying and selling of such things. But I didn't adhere to this idea of scalping one's enemies and believed any who did were the savages, white or red, black or otherwise. It was a barbaric act that I wanted no part of.

As I stood looking at the resting place of the two fallen warriors I said to them, "Ye gave it yer all, boys, that's fer sure. May you have it easy in the next life. No hard feelings." Anyone within earshot would have only thought they had heard a whispered prayer for the dead.

Even though it felt wrong at the time, I also knew I had no other choice than to uncover and search the two for whatever they might have that I needed. It was pure survival, and I did it with respect for the two men. In my search, I found a deerskin sack full of jerked venison and some pemmican, some dried berries, one knife, and a small gold trinket was all I found useful. The little gold piece would bring a decent price at rendezvous but the thought of selling it never entered my mind. Curiosity *did* enter my mind, however.

"Well! Still no powder, no shot, but at least I got more food for a few days, Time to go!" I grunted when I shouldered my pack once more and I felt a wave of weariness. I took a bite of jerky and started to chew as I walked on in the direction of the secret pass.

It was going to be a long night, and cold. It seemed the temperature had dropped twenty degrees or so since sundown, but with snow falling there was no other choice. I was going to have to pick up the pace! I began to run. Just a loping jog really, but I would cover twice the distance as long as I didn't put a foot in a hole and get a broken leg out of the deal.

After about an hour, I had traveled approximately four miles from where I had my fight with the Indians, winding through thickets of spruce and around clumps of junipers and sagebrush. It was quite dark as there was only a sliver of the moon visible through the clouds that showered the snow. I slowed to a walk again to catch my breath and thought I heard something in the brush that wasn't right. I kept up a steady walk. I thought I heard footsteps behind me off to the right in the trees. I pretended to take no notice of this but loosened my knife in its sheath as I walked, just in case.

When I came to a little gully I stopped suddenly and took my pack off and pretended to look in it while I listened intently to the night. Nothing. I took out a piece of jerky and cut a piece of it off with my knife and then closed up my pack again. I must just be still feeling paranoid from having been chased for days by the Indians.

As I chewed on the jerky let out a little chuckle. "Days . . . more like *weeks.*"

Wait . . . there it was again! A shuffling almost in the brush. It was very faint as if in the distance but there was definitely *something* out there that wasn't natural to the environment. I stopped chewing and again listened intently, I even stopped breathing for a period, but this time in vain. I heard nothing.

After what seemed a long time, though in reality only a few minutes, and not having heard anything more, I once again shouldered my pack and took my bearings. This time carrying Long Stick in one hand and my knife still in the other. My little encounter with the ghostly sounds had given me a breather and I again began to run. The snow was coming down harder and thicker now and I still had a long way to go.

Chapter 7

The sun started to peek over the mountains to the east and glistened off the fresh snow covering the valley floor. The air smelled fresh and clean with a hint of pine and spruce that hung all around in the air.

Tom awoke suddenly and found Long Walker was already tending to the fire and had a nice little blaze going. There was a well-used cast iron pan on the fire getting hot while Long chunked up the last of the bacon into it to fry.

I wish I had about four eggs to go with that, Tom thought to himself, but all he said was, "Got coffee goin' yet?"

"Coffee there." Long pointed with his knife. "Hot," he added.

"You use up all the sugar yet?" Tom blurted a little more jokingly than anything. Long just grunted and tossed him the sack with the sugar in it.

"When did you get in camp?" Tom inquired.

"Long after dark. Moon was starting to go down," Walker replied. "I go look all over for a way to cross but I find nothing."

"Well, we'll start at the bottom here and work our way up to the top again. I'll pull all the traps this time, empty or otherwise, while we look again in daylight for any sign." Tom shivered and pulled his coat tighter around himself while he reached for the coffee pot. "I *know* that this is the last place Silas came to. Either he crossed here or he left his body here and went on to the hereafter."

"Huh," came from Long as he nodded in agreement.

"You got biscuits goin' yet?" Tom asked, knowing the answer. While the Indian was a decent cook with most things, he couldn't make a decent biscuit to save his life.

"You want biscuit, you make!" was Walker's reply. Tom just chuckled and poured his coffee, smelling the bacon frying in the pan.

"And don't burn that bacon neither, ya ignernt savage!" Tom said with a smile.

Walker said nothing. He knew Tom's sense of humor and in all honestly enjoyed his little jabs now and then. They made him feel like a brother. Long's brother, Little Eagle, was the same way, always chiding him in a humorous tone. Of course, he held his brow furrowed and made sure Tom saw no evidence of this on his face.

Tom decided to skip the biscuits this morning and sat sipping his coffee, lost in thought. He was going to have to talk with Silas if he ever saw him alive again. This secretive way of doing things was going to have to change! He knew Silas had good reasons to keep his ideas under his hat, but Tom had begun to trust him implicitly and he needed Silas to know he could be trusted too! Tom was no babe in the woods and if they were going to have a true partnership, Silas was going to have to start sharing some of the responsibility for his own safety and let Tom shoulder some of the load, dangerous though it may be. He knew Silas would hate to lose a man that he had sent into danger, but that was the nature of this business. And by God, it was time Silas understood Tom 'The Headhunter' Sweet knew it as well!

"*Tom*"

If Silas didn't show up in a day or two . . .

"*Tom.*"

He was going to have to find a way . . .

"*TOM*!" Long poked him in the shoulder with a plate of bacon.

"Sorry, Long," he said quietly as he took the plate. "Kinda got lost in my thoughts there for a few." He let his voice trail off into the breeze and put a piece of bacon in his mouth to chew. Long just nodded and poured himself a cup of the strong black coffee and reached for the sugar sack.

When the two men were done eating, they both silently began to prepare for the day's chore. The storm had been a light one and there was only a thin covering of new snow on the ground. It was nothing that would hamper them in their efforts or slow their progress in the least.

As the day progressed, Tom took seven beavers from his trap line of twenty sets up and down the valley. Not encouraging as far as business goes, but his mind was far from business today.

If Silas did not return . . . business would be far from a major concern anyway.

When he had skinned out the last of the beavers, he began to help Long look for sign of where Silas had got off to. The snow made everything look pretty much the same. Though it was still overcast and threatening to snow more, he found a large stone on which to sit, load his pipe, and smoke while looking over the valley below.

Had it not been for the circumstances he was in, he might have called it beautiful.

The high mountain lake covered about five acres, though it was covered with ice and snow at the moment. It was encircled sparsely with twisted cedars and high mountain pines. The terrain sloped down and away following a little stream that flowed down from the mountain lake. At his back were thousand-foot cliffs that walled the valley in on three sides leaving only one entrance to the valley far below. Aspens were clawing their leafless limbs toward any sunlight coming from the sky. Where there wasn't the dark green of the evergreens there was only white below, until one reached the foothills and started to open up onto the high desert plains.

Even though it had snowed, Tom could still see the little beaver ponds and streams that traced their way down the valley. As he smoked his pipe, he kept looking at the terrain over again and again searching for any sign his eyes had missed before. He just *knew* there had to be a way to cross over to get to the other side.

Some movement caught his eye off to his left, against the rock face. A mountain lion was emerging from his den. The skin would bring a nice price at rendezvous and the meat would come in handy as well. He didn't have a male mountain lion skull yet so he would have to remember where this cave was and—

His pipe drooped from his teeth and slowly he reached a hand up to take it from his mouth, his mind racing, whirling with thought. All at once it hit him and he knew the answer! He quickly tapped out his pipe into the snow and hopped down from the rock on which he had perched and took off at a quick lope. Then faster he ran towards where he knew Long Walker was in search of tracks.

He *knew* Silas had come this way and now he knew where he had gone! And *how*!

Chapter 8

I awoke in a world of pain and darkness. My head felt as though the weight of a mountain was crushing down upon it. When I moved, my ribs as well would crack and shoot stabbing pains throughout my body. One leg was stiff and painful, swollen to what felt like twice its normal size. When I tried to roll to one side in order to try to stand, I nearly passed out again from the pain.

I could only lie there and *Holy HELL! What the f—*

"Do not move Seniore," came a voice from the darkness startling me. "You may well undo what I have-a done to save you," the voice told me.

"Who . . . are you? Where . . . is this place? What . . . happened?" My voice would only come in short bursts of pain. It smelled damp and earthy, and through the haze of pain and confusion, it came to me. "THE CAVE!"

"Yes, Seniore," came the voice again. "You are in a cave, the only place I could bring you to escape the snowstorm," it explained.

"Who are you?" I whispered this time. I knew that accent; I had heard it before back on the riverboats of Missouri country. The voice was Italian.

"I am Father Antonio Levetti," the voice explained. "You have had a bad fall in the night," the voice went on. "And you can a call me Father Levi, Or just-a Levi if you are not-a catholic, of course."

"A *priest*?" I said that too loud and immediately regretted it. "What the devil is a priest doing a way up in these mountains?" I managed through a clenched jaw.

"In time, Seniore, in time I will tell you all," Father Levi replied.

I heard the tapping of flint against steel and saw sparks a few feet away in the darkness. Soon the sparks turned to a faint glow in the hands of a man, but what I saw in the firelight did not look like a man!

As the glow formed into flames, and the flames grew to a fire on the cave floor, I saw the shape of a big black bear start to take shape.

"For now, we-a need heat!" Levi went on, "And-a light, and you need water and food! You have had a rough go and you-a need to regain your-a strength!"

As the flames licked at the wood the bear shape was feeding it, the light began to grow and I began to see the shape of a bear transform into the shape of a huge man with a thick. black beard and a shaggy mane of hair, long and unkempt and wild. The priest was dressed in a thick bearskin coat and a hat that was made from the head of a bear, which explained my earlier vision of talking to a bear. Dressed as he was, he didn't *look* like a priest. Under his coat, he dressed in animal skins of varying sizes roughly sewn together, or maybe unskillfully made more likely.

"My pack!" Damn, that hurt to say. "I need my pack! I have medicine in it that will help," I explained a little quieter.

"Ah, yes!" the big man responded. "I gathered up what I could find from-a where you fell, but your pack was-a broke open so maybe some-a things be lost, no?"

I described the little wooden box with the brass latch on the front. "Were you able to recover that?" I asked. "And was there anything in it?"

"Ah, yes!" Levi said while he got up and retrieved my pack and brought it to me. The fire was going nicely now and gave more than enough light to see this was *not* the cave I had used to come through from the other side of the peaks. *Or is it?* I thought. *Maybe there's another entrance on this side.*

I rifled through my pack, one-armed, as my other was bound tight against my ribs. After some cussing under my breath, I found my little tea box and my tin cup. "Is there water?" I asked the priest.

The big man only nodded and tossed me a full water skin.

I began to remember more of the events of the previous day as I put the water and tea over the fire with a groan of pain. As I had come to a rise in the foothills that led to the cave, I came to a washout in the trail. When there was no snow, it was an easy hop across the gap. The little canyon was deep but not too wide. I remembered thinking I should try to go around it but had decided against it and tried to jump it to save time.

In jumping the little ravine, I could remember now through the throbbing pains, I had slipped in the snow and fallen over thirty feet down into the ravine. How this so-called priest found me down there in the middle of a snowstorm, I didn't know. But I know if he hadn't, I would surely have frozen to death before too long.

"I guess I need to thank you for saving my life. When that starts to boil, please give it back." I couldn't sit up any longer and leaned back against the cave wall. "I don't think I can lean that far again and I will need to drink it while it's hot. Half of the medicine is in it being warm."

Father Levi said nothing.

I went on, "But please, tell me, who are you and why are you alone here in these mountains?"

"Soon my son," was the priest's soft reply. My eyes began to close with exhaustion. "When you're-a strong enough to stay awake while I-a do."

Chapter 9

The next day, Tom was sitting on his saddle in camp, smoking his pipe and drinking coffee while cooking a venison roast on the fire. It was near sunset, and he had been scraping and drying hides all day and stretching them onto willow hoops. It was a task that required little thinking, so he had been thinking of how to go about the next couple of days. He was going to have to hunt for the lion tomorrow while Long Walker gathered up the rest of the crews and brought them in for a search party. He didn't expect to see them until about midday or even early evening the next day.

He had convinced Long to take one of the horses even though (as his name suggested) he preferred to walk or run everywhere he went. "It'll just take less time," he had told the Ute. "And time is something we don't have much of right now!"

He hoped it was not *already* too late.

The coffee pot boiled over and sizzled and spat on the hot coals. Tom swore, "Damn! No more daydreamin', ya old fool!" he admonished himself. "One of these days, some redskin will have yer hair before ya even know he's in camp!" He quickly grabbed the hot pot off the fire, burning his fingers slightly as he did so. "Ow, ow, ow!"

While he was turning the spit of meat over the fire, he heard a twig snap in the distance and then a familiar voice cry out, "HALLOO THE CAMP! Comin' in'!"

And another, "Don't shoot now, ya mangy ol' cuss, we are two who wanna keep our heads on our shoulders!" the voice chuckled.

"Come on in, boys! I been expectin' ya!" Tom ignored the headhunter jibe. "Got supper almost done and we got some talkin' to do!" He then pulled a knife from his belt and cut a slice of the roast and took it between his teeth to chew. Out of the mist of the evening mountain air, the two voices began to take shape as they rode into camp.

Saul Younger and his partner, Cole Stevens, were both from the Missouri country. Hearty rawboned men of the Ozark mountains. Both were excellent horsemen and marksmen; hunters born and bred for the hard living of the mountains. Saul was a tall, hawk-faced man who stood over six feet tall and was as skinny as a rail. He dressed in white buckskins when it snowed (like it was doing now) and wore a coat made from woolen trade blankets, white also with four colored stripes on it. It was his pride from the rendezvous the year before. On his head, he wore a cap made of beaver fur, with a hawk feather tied into the side.

Cole, on the other hand, was a shorter man standing about five and a half feet tall but weighed well over 200 pounds of thick corded muscle. He had powerful hands on thick, tree trunk arms, and a head almost too small for his body in comparison. He too wore buckskins, but his were a smokey yellowish color, and he had painted black stripes down the legs at odd angles, to help him hide in the shadows, he told people when they asked. He wore an old-fashioned canvas fringed hunting jacket he had dyed green and a matching woolen cap like the French men wore up north.

It was rumored that Cole had killed the wrong man for the right reason and had to flee Missouri country with his partner, Saul. They had decided to head for the Rocky Mountains on the Canadian side of the border to escape prosecution in a land far away and still very wild. This was where they had met up with Silas and Tom at a rendezvous. This was their first year working with them but had already proven themselves to be good, honest, hard-working men, and were fitting in well.

They both carried their rifles in the crooks of their arms as they rode into camp. After dismounting and tying their horses to the picket line just outside of camp, they strode in and squatted by the fire.

As usual, Cole spoke first as he uncocked his rifle, "So, what's all the commotion, Tom? Walker only said that ya wanted us to come in, and fast, and that you would explain."

"Ya shouldn't go traipsing around with yer rifle cocked, Cole," Tom winked at the Missourian. "Ya may end up shootin' the wrong man that-a-way!" Tom pointed out.

"Wouldn't be the first time!" Cole responded. "But, ya know, old habits are hard to break. Too used to bein' a wanted man!"

"I suppose." Tom just chuckled and pointed to the roast on the spit. "Break out yer knives boys, we can eat while we talk."

"I hope you cook better'n Cole does!" Saul grunted as he drug up a small barrel to sit on. "We been eating burnt meat and dry biscuit for nigh on two months now!"

Cole grabbed his chest as if wounded. "Oh, ow! That hurt. We could be eating it half-raw with *no* biscuit if I let you do the cookin'!" Cole had just kicked himself a clear spot and sat on the ground on a horse blanket. "*This*, on the other hand, looks pretty good!" he said as he reached for his knife. He cut a slice of the meat and began to blow on it. Saul took out a couple of pieces of hardtack and put a chunk of meat between them and set it on a rock to cool.

"So, Tom, what's this news?" Saul blurted suddenly. "Why you pullin' us off the traps only part way done with the season? Who died?"

"Silas is late . . . two weeks late," Tom explained. "I'm worried somethin' happened to him!"

Cole, chewing on a mouthful of meat, chimed in, "Silas can take care of himself, we all know that., Why you think somethin' happened to him?"

Tom cut another hunk of meat off the roast and held it on his knife tip to cool while he answered.

"Dunno, call it a hunch, I suppose, but he's never been this late before! " Tom went on "He told me he would be on a scoutin' trip into some new country *BEFORE* the snows block the passes." Gesturing around them at the layer of white on the ground. "And that leads me to believe he crossed over to the east side of these here mountains, and as we all know the Blackfeet and Crow don't take well to trespassers. And as far south as we are there might be Kioway and Comanche too, according to Long."

The two Missourians listened, chewing on their meal as Tom went on, "Hell, look at what we had to do to get rights to hunt and trap *this* side!" Both men nodded their agreement. "Well, the high passes are snowed in now, and Silas ain't back. That *could* mean two things: either he's dead, or he's trapped on the other side till spring, which we all know means about the same thing!" He paused here for a moment to shove another slice of meat into his mouth. Then, with his mouth full, he began again, "But, I don't think he *went* over any pass! I think he found a way *through* the mountain itself!"

The other two men looked at each other a moment before Cole finally asked, "What are you talkin' bout 'through' the mountain?"

Tom didn't answer right away but got up, opened a small pine box and pulled a crockery jug out, and sat back down by the fire. After he uncorked it and took a pull for himself he passed it to Saul, who did the same.

"I think there's a cave that goes all the way through to the other side," Tom said. "And I think I found it meself!" He took a moment to measure the looks on his companions' faces before going on.

Both men were silent for a moment. Saul took another stiff drink and tried to hand the jug to Cole, who waved him off and put some meat in his mouth instead.

"So, where's this cave?" Saul asked. "And when we goin' lookin'?"

. "This is the valley Silas has been keeping secret for us this year, and the cave is up near the lake at the top near those cliffs," Tom pointed as he explained. "And were goin' once Long gets back with the rest of the boys in the other crews. But first, we got a mountain lion to kill."

Saul handed the jug back to Tom and chuckled. "It's always somethin' ain't it?"

"Hell, Tom, ya coulda said so," added Cole. "What ya got in mind?"

While Cole reached for the jug over the fire, Tom began, "Well, here's what I figger . . ."

Chapter 10

I opened my eyes to the now familiar sight of the huge priest sitting by the fire, reading a bible and praying.

When he noticed I had awakened, he closed the bible and asked me, "So, how are you-a feeling after your-a sleep, my son?"

I didn't answer right away but sat up with a grunt of pain. I sat for a moment, testing my limbs and trying to relieve some of the stiffness before I finally said, "I believe I will live, Levi. Thanks to you." Even I could hear the twinge of pain in my voice as I strained to breathe.

The priest stood up and retreated further back into the cave for a moment, again looking like a big black bear walking on his hind legs in the firelight. When he returned, he had a bundle with him which, when he unwrapped it, turned out to be a plucked turkey he then put on a spit of green wood to place on the fire. "Thanks to God, you mean?"

"Where did you get that?" I asked. "I see no musket, no bow. How did you bring down a turkey?"

The priest just smiled, showing yellowed and broken teeth. "Same as David brought down Goliath!" he said, producing a sling from the pocket of his bear coat.

Impressive, I thought to myself, but only nodded at the priest and asked, "How long have I been here?"

"Two days and nights, now. Between your injuries from your fall, and your-a recent journeys, you-a needed your rest!" He went on to explain my knee had only been dislocated, not broken as I had feared. I swore it hurt just as much as if it *had* been broken. Still, I was relieved. A whiff of smoke caught my nose and made me cough, causing me to wince in pain again.

"Do not-a push yourself too fast, my son," chided the priest. "You still need-a much more rest to heal your injuries. A-too much a-too soon will only make-a them worse!"

"I have little time for healing Levi," I explained. "I have to cross to the other side of this mountain before the way is blocked with snow. I have people waiting for me on the other side that can help me. I have . . ." I let the thought trail off there as I didn't want to reveal too much. I only had this man's word as to who and what he was, and in the wild, trust does not come immediately.

"Yes, yes, I know of-a your, say, activities here and know you have caches of-a furs you have collected here." Levi finished my thought as if it were his own!

"Wait! It was you!"

"I *also* know of your-a escape from the Crow camp."

Now I had some understanding of the ghostly rustlings I had been hearing the last few days of my escape from the Indians. "You have been trailin' me! That's what I heard behind me! YOU!"

"Yes-a my son, I have, I admit," The priest confirmed.

"Why didn't you just show yourself? I would have welcomed friendly company!" I sat back in new waves of pain from the effort the conversation was taking.

"I wish to-a remain alive, Seniore," The priest responded. "I could a not-a . . . interfere with the business of the Crow if-a I wish to remain-a their friend now, can I?"

Now *that* made me stiff!

"In fact, I-a risk much in-a helping you-a now!"

I sat for a moment just letting the words I had just heard sink into my pain muddled mind. It was going to take a moment to absorb the impact of what I had just heard!

The bird on the fire began rendering its juices, sizzling in the coals underneath. It was beginning to start to smell quite good in the cave and I realized how hungry I was. "Is there water?" I asked "Of course" the priest responded and tossed me a water skin, full, and pointed to another. "Where there is snow, there is water" the big man shrugged.

I could no longer hold back my obvious curiosity. "How did you come to be here, Levi? It's a wild place for a man alone. Especially a white man in the company of Indians that will scalp or kill any other white man they come across."

The big man only turned his head to look me in the eye. It was a long moment like he was measuring me for something. Sizing me up behind his eyes. When he did turn away, he asked me, "You know the-a Spanish used to own all this, yes?"

I nodded. I had heard the stories of Cortez and others, who had conquered this land for the Spanish and the atrocities they had imposed on the natives in Mexico.

"This used to all be Mexico," The priest said while tending to the fire which was growing dim. "I-ah came with a party of-a Franciscan Monks from Mexico, where I was in seminary as a boy. I didn't . . . agree with how the-a Spanish treated the people here, and I-a wished to help them. I decided I was going to stay and-a minister to these lost children of God when the-a Spanish left. I have-a been here ever since."

I did a short bit of figuring in my head and the number of years this man had been in these mountains was staggering! Alone and in the wilds with Indians around, hostile to every other white man they saw. Why would they let this man stay unharmed?

"I was taken in a raid by the Crow. Since I would not-a fight, I was not-a killed outright, possibly because I am a man of God, no?" the priest continued as he made the sign of the cross. "Perhaps they believed it-a would a be bad for-a them if they harmed me."

I only nodded and continued to listen, eyeing the turkey cooking on the fire as it was almost done.

"In time, they released me into the-a village as a free man. They found I had-a knowledge of medicine and healing and soon I was given the name 'White Medicine Bear.'"

"*You* are 'White Medicine Bear'? The legend of the White Medicine Bear is supposed to be some mythical creature, half bear and half . . . Ah, I see now."

"Yes, my son, and it is because of that legend that even the Crow allow me to exist here," Levi explained.

As we talked, the big man would now and again turn the bird on the spit, never looking at me directly. Every once in a while, he would hum a little tune quietly to himself when there were pauses in conversation. I thought, *Years of wandering alone in a wilderness will generate quirky habits in any man. Even a man of God.*

After some pause, I had to break the silence, "I feel I must warn you Levi, at the other end of this cave is a mountain lion's den. Perhaps it would be best to move soon, the cat may know the way through. In fact, I am quite sure of it!"

"Son, this-a cave has-a no other end," Levi replied still looking into the fire. "Perhaps I have misjudged your injuries. Do you a have any bad pain in-a your head?"

"No, no. My head is fine. This must not be the cave I thought it was."

A few moments passed before Levi answered. "I know of the cave you-a speak of." Levi nodded as he took the turkey off the fire and set it on a large rock nearby to cool. "It is not-a more than a half a day's walk from-a here. And-a you are correct, my son, it *is* the residence of a-one big a cat!" The big man looked me in the eyes again. "You mean-a to tell-a me, you came-a through the lion's den with-a no a problem? I am amazed!"

"I have my ways, Levi, as do you. I have my ways."

Chapter 11

"Missing? How ya mean he's MISSING?" Samuel was incredulous with disbelief. "Silas knows these mountains better'n the back of his hand! How can he be MISSING?" he exclaimed.

"The Headhunter tell me find the Scot man and tell him this, 'Silas Horn is late and may be missing, we go to look for him as soon as Scot man can bring the Red Hair brothers to secret valley,'" Walker explained. "I do not know how Silas can be lost but if Headhunter say we go look, we go," he added.

"Well, the McNeils are in the next little valley north, just before the river. I'll go and collect 'em and bring them to Silas' valley. Long Walker can go and tell the Headhunter it is done!" Samuel told the scout. Long turned his horse to the south while Samuel turned north and kicked his horse to a lope.

If Silas was missing there was a great need for concern. Being late was one thing; Silas had been late on many occasions. But, if Tom 'The Headhunter' Sweet thought Silas was missing, there was indeed a need for concern. And haste! All their fortunes and futures depended on Silas Horn!

He was the one who had shown them this new territory rich with furs. He was the one who had taught them how to cut their initial cost and investment nearly in half with his tent designs. *And* he was the one who had the contact to sell the furs at top dollar at the rendezvous! Any of the rest of them may only get two-thirds of what Silas could get!

Samuel thought as he rode, and he rode hard! Through the pines and over the grassy mountain meadows his path lay. It was two days since the wide skies had blanketed the foothills with a dusting of snow. For two days, the sun had been melting that thin blanket, and most of it in the lower elevations was gone now. This made traveling a little easier and quicker. He just hoped to find the McNeil brothers quickly and get them mounted and on the way to go help with the search. They may have to all travel far into the night.

After about an hour of hard riding, he reined in his sturdy little mountain mustang and let him have his head at a walk for a while to catch his breath.

His thoughts went back to the day he had met Silas Horn for the first time. They met at a rendezvous on the Umpquah River in the Oregon Territory. They both worked for the American Fur Company at that time and Silas was buying supplies and asking around about a trader with a supply of canvas or sailcloth.

"Sailcloth?" Samuel blurted out. "Why would ye need a supply of sail cloth when yer goin' in the mountains trappin'? Ya gonna *sail* upriver into the mountains? Or ya quittin' and goin' to sea instead?" he had asked Silas as a bit of a joke.

Silas only looked the crusty ol' Scot in the eye and responded, "I'm quittin' the Company and goin' out on my own, and I got some ideas." The Scot looked at him quizzically, so Silas went on. "I'm going to the Rocky Mountains this year. There's valleys there full o' beaver and other furs, all for the taking. Places where no white man has been yet. I want to see those places! The French and Canadians, not to mention the English, have overrun this territory and these beaver will soon be trapped out!"

"Sure, yer right there, man." Samuel nodded in agreement.

Silas continued, "I heard of a place that's ripe for trapping, and maybe for trading with the Indians there to make the work easier as well. But it's going to take a completely different way of doing things to do it. It's gonna be dangerous, I'll reckon, but I believe worth it too! I'm going to go and take my chances, anyway!"

Silas had impressed Samuel and he wanted to learn more, so when Silas invited him back to his camp to talk more and pass a jug he wholeheartedly agreed. He was further impressed by Silas' camp. It was in a little grove of trees and berry vines, a little ways off from the main body of the camp. If Silas had not led him directly into the camp, he may have walked right by it, never knowing it was there.

There was no big white wall tent and no pavilion like many of the traders. There was no pointed tipi like many of the trappers were starting to use, adapted from the native shelter used in the mountains and plains all across this new land. These were also made of the white or smokey gray canvas available in the ports and trading posts, but they stuck out like a sore thumb among the greenery of the environment.

Instead, his tent was staked out low to the ground in a diamond-shaped lean-to, tied to a sapling in the grove of trees and bushes. Silas had made sure his camp wouldn't be seen by staining it with dirt, grass, mud, and soot, to blend in with the surrounding vegetation. Another hung between two trees with a canvas hammock suspended beneath it, also stained so well it blended in with the trees.

"Damn near invisible if ya ain't lookin', ain't it!" he exclaimed quite suddenly. Silas went on to explain how each could be tied around a common pole in a star shape one for each man; collectively around one fire when camping together, or for each to take with them when working alone as many did in those days. Five of these together in a star shape was perfect for a four-man team with an extra to cover supplies. Samuel agreed a camp like this could go virtually undetected in the rough mountain country. He also knew quite well the value of going unseen in some of the territory Silas planned to go into. Samuel deemed Silas a man of intelligence and wit, and one ahead of his time.

After a couple more hours of riding, Samuel came to the stream where the McNeil brothers were working this week and turned his mount upstream. It wasn't long before he came upon David up to his knees in the icy water of a beaver pond tying a scent stick to his trap set.

"David, where's yer brother?" he shouted from some distance away. "We got urgent business elsewhere!"

Chris stepped out from behind a tree and shouted, "BANG, yer dead old man! I figgered I'd stay outta sight, in case who we heard a comin' weren't so friendly as you!"

Samuel ignored the comment. "Yous two need to get packed up for a week and come wit' me!"

"What business ya mean, Sam?" David asked as the Scot got closer to where he was standing, dripping from the knees down.

"We're goin' lookin' fer Silas! He's far too late to just be late and Tom is worried somethin' ill may have become of him."

"When we goin'?" was David's only question.

"Tom's got a bit of dirty work to do wit' those Missouri boys before we go a-lookin'. But you two need to be ready to go as soon as possible. And get dried off too, we may be riding into the night and it's a bit chill."

"Aye. it is!" David agreed. "Come now, Chris, me lad! Seems ya git yer wish. We got a huntin' to do!"

Samuel explained further on the way to their camp, and while they prepared for the next few days. Within two hours, all their furs and extra gear were cached safely and they were packed and riding south with Samuel.

Chapter 12

Back in the secret valley, the rest of the crew was sitting around a campfire in a new camp. This one was about halfway up the valley to the cave in a grove of aspen. Being experienced and seasoned outdoorsmen and operating under the assumption that this cat had two entrances to its lair as most do, the men had pooled all their resources (and traps) to catch this one mountain lion.

"You sure this is gonna work, Abe?" Tom asked. "You know more than the rest of us about catchin' these cats, I'll grant ya, but just settin' traps all around and waiting?" He shook his head slightly. "I jus' don't think we got that kinda time!"

Abraham just smiled, showing his yellowed teeth, and patted his bow. "Ain't all we been doin'," Abe explained. "While y'all was settin' traps around, I shot us a deer!" He reached up to scratch under his hat for a moment then went on, "I hung it up in a tree once I took a haunch for us there." He pointed to his pack horse. "Now, I'll admit a mountain cat would rather hunt its dinner rather than take a handout, but I'm bettin' since its winter and we ain't seen much game around, this one's hungry enough to take the bait. If it even looks out its door it's gonna smell that deer a'hangin' in that tree and gonna wanna take a taste."

Tom had been nodding through half of Abe's explanation and now broke in, "Yes, yes, the smell of blood in the air, I get it. But we're still sittin' here waiting for maybe, instead of goin' huntin'!" Tom stood up in frustration and began pacing back and forth by the fire. "I was really hoping to be in that cave already!"

"Trust me, Tom, ya don't want in that cave less'n yer sure there ain't no cat in it! You don't want no part of a cat trapped in its own cave!" argued the lanky Missourian.

"Ya got a point there," Tom conceded. They had had this discussion before and Abe had won that debate as well. The fact they were all feeling anxious, just sitting and waiting, had to be ignored for the moment. Everyone was a bit jittery waiting for their traps to spring or for their remaining associates to show up to help.

Without a word, Long Walker stood up, took his rifle, and walked off into the woods. No one needed to ask where he was going, or warn him of the danger of the lion, he was Ute and this was where he had lived most of his life. He was more an expert in this land than any of them. Plus, asking would do no good anyway; he wouldn't answer. He rarely did.

Cole broke the lingering silence, "Welp! Biscuits are done! We got bacon and coffee . . . we may as well cook up that haunch of muley that Abe brought too! If nothin' else, when we do go we can take it with us."

"Yer probably right," Tom agreed. "Eight men is a lot to feed on the trail, might be nice to not have to stop and hunt and cook."

Abe got up and went to go retrieve the leg of deer while the rest of the men took turns dipping their biscuits in the bacon grease or making a sandwich with them. Abe and Cole finished skinning the deer leg and drove a green limb through it to use as a spit over the fire. It wasn't until the venison was almost done that anyone spoke again.

"Okay, I'm just gonna ask what we're all thinkin'!" Saul blurted suddenly. "What if we don't find him? Or find him dead?"

Tom was standing some distance off, smoking his pipe. When he realized they were all waiting for him to answer, he tapped out his pipe and took a couple of steps closer. He cleared his throat and tried his best to sound like he knew what to do. "We do the best we can the rest of the season, business as usual. We go to rendezvous with the traders and sell for what we can and do it again next season!"

"Look, let's not start thinkin' the worst!" Cole broke in. "Let's just think about the job ahead for now and go find him!"

"You're right," Saul admitted. "It's just hard to *not* think about it."

Chapter 13

Black Coyote stopped for a moment on a butte overlooking the valley where his village lay waiting for him. This was the winter camp his people had used for as far back as anyone could remember. He thought for a moment about whom he must speak to about the last few days' events. White Eyes was going to be disappointed, to say the least. Dull Knife was his only surviving son, so this news would be hard on the Old One.

It would also be hard on Yellow Horse; brother of Running Elk. Losing a member of the tribe was hard on all the people. Everyone was needed and dear and no one was expendable. Too few were left after so many battles with their enemies, the harsh winters, and this new sickness the whites brought with them that was starting to affect the people as well.

As he thought, he looked over the hills and mountains that had always been here for his people. Forests of pine and cedar, juniper, hemlock, and aspen. The snow-capped peaks to the west, the great river in its canyon carving its path down to the plains.

Everything was as it should be, how it always had been. But now, for some reason he could not identify, it seemed different. Something was not right. He could feel a difference as one can feel the change in the wind as a storm was coming.

He turned his nose into the wind; he didn't smell anything different than normal, just the sweet grass and sage, the scent of pine. He looked over his homelands slowly. There was nothing but the foothills covered in a light dusting of snow. Everything looked as it always had. He strained his ears but heard only the wind rustling the grass at his feet and rushing through the treetops. The cry of an eagle came to his ears, then the distant answer of its mate.

All was as it should be . . . but for some reason, he was filled with fear, an impending sense of dread for his people and their way of life.

Perhaps it was this trespassing white he had been chasing. Maybe it was the words of White Medicine Bear echoing in his ears. Whatever it was, Black Coyote didn't like the feeling.

After quite some time standing and looking, he decided it was time to deliver his news. White Eyes and the council members would need to decide what to do now. This white now knew the location of their sacred valley. They must decide whether to stay or find another home before the next winter came.

"Where one white man goes many others follow," White Medicine Bear had said, and his words stung in Black Coyote's mind.

When he got within earshot of the camp he shouted his greeting, "Caw! Caw! Caw!" to let the people know Black Coyote had returned!

The boys guarding the horse herd were the first to greet him, but he ignored their pestering confused questions. What had happened? Where were his friends and all the horses? He just walked past them in silence. He had to speak to White Eyes first, the boys could wait. Among shouts of greetings from those he passed, he soon came to find White Eyes sitting by the fire outside his tipi, as he always did when it was warm out. As always, the blind old man greeted him first as though he could see him coming.

"You return alone, Black Coyote," he began. "Tell me, where are your brothers, or what has befallen them?"

Black Coyote found he couldn't even look into a blind old man's eyes as he responded, "They are dead, Old One," he replied respectfully. He knelt and took the old man's hand and held it to his chest. "And before the beat of my heart stops, I will avenge them both!" he vowed.

The old man nodded slowly. "I know you will, as I would if I were a young man."

"I will take three men and leave in the morning and hunt him until—"

"No!" the old man stopped him mid-sentence. "There are other things you must know. There is other news since you left. Give word to the Elders as you have me of what has happened and ask them to gather at dusk for a talk."

"I will," was all Black Coyote could say as he got up to do so.

After he delivered White Eyes' message to the Elders, he told Yellow Horse of the death of his brother. They talked for a while about vengeance and how they should strike off on their own to go after this white. In the end, they agreed it was a trail long gone cold, and this time the white had gotten away. Going back up into the mountains now would be a waste of time at the least, and dangerous at the most.

When he entered the tipi of Fox Flower, she greeted him with a warm embrace. "You have been gone many days, I feared you would not return," she spoke into his chest. "In my dreams, you were killed . . ."

"Shhhh . . . I am here," Black Coyote said quietly and held her tighter to him. "Feel me, I am here."

After a few silent moments, Fox Flower pulled away and looked at him, poking his ribs. "You need food, you look hungry. I killed a pheasant this morning, I will cook that for you."

Black Coyote said nothing as he stripped off his weapons and put them in their place in his woman's home. He sat on his bearskin by the fire and let out an exhausted sigh. For a while, he stared into the flames searching for any sign his fears were unfounded.

Fox Flower propped the bird over the flames to roast and then brought him a gourd with water. "What will happen now?" she asked quietly.

He sipped the water slowly, feeling its power rejuvenate his spirit a little before he answer, "Only the creator can say." He paused for a moment before he went on, "But I fear there is a change coming for our people. Life is going to become very hard soon. Many may not survive. We may not survive."

"You have been listening too much to White Medicine Bear," his wife scolded him playfully.

Nodding slowly he answered, "That may be, but it is not just that. I had a vision a few nights ago," Black Coyote spoke quietly into the firelight. "In my vision, our people were scattered and left to walk alone in the mountains. Starving, hunted, lost, and dying. White men lived where our people had always lived. They killed our people while they smiled as a friend . . ." his voice drifted off into whispers. Then silence again.

After some time, Fox Flower touched his hand and he blinked in surprise. He looked at his woman and sighed. "We cannot defeat the whites, they are like the snow in winter, one after another until the land is covered. Soon there will be no place for the people."

Fox Flower didn't know what to say as she cut up the pheasant and gave Black Coyote his part.

They ate in silence.

Chapter 14

Tom awoke to see Long Walker setting the coffee pot on the fire to boil. He sat up quickly, knowing what the scout's presence in the camp meant. Either the cat had been trapped or had escaped and was still at large in the valley. He coughed as a puff of smoke found his lungs while he rubbed the sleep out of his eyes with his knuckles.

"Well? Did it work?" he asked the Ute.

"The bait is gone," answered Long. "So is one trap," he added.

Tom's face lost its color as he realized what this meant. All they had succeeded in doing was creating a much more dangerous enemy! The cat had gotten to the bait unscathed but in dragging the meat back to its lair, it had been caught in a trap. In its fierce fight to escape, the cat had uprooted the trap and now was gone; the trap still on its paw!

The game had just gotten more dangerous, as now they had a wounded and angry cat that had retreated into its cave where they needed to go. Tom swore bitterly under his breath and turned to see the others now walking into camp as well. "You boys are gonna love this!" he shouted.

Samuel broke in, "We heard!" he exclaimed. "And I for one nominate Abe to go in that cave first, now!"

"I'll second that!" Abe responded. "I coulda swore that set-up woulda worked! *Always* has on them cats back home!"

"Well, no use tryin' to lay blame now it's done!" Saul spoke up. "I suggest we keep our heads and git to what's gotta be done now!"

The rest nodded and mumbled their grim agreement, and they began to prepare for what was to come.

Soon the coffee was bubbling and beaver and venison were cooking over the fire, and a bit of a meat stew Long had put together. Once they had all eaten and finished their coffee, nearly all at once, they got up and gathered their gear. Long poured the last of the coffee into the fire to douse it and kicked the remains apart.

They left the horses to fend for themselves. It was a lush little valley and they were confident they wouldn't stray too far for a while. They were tough little horses and knew the mountains and could survive the next few weeks for themselves just fine.

Silently, they made their way up the valley to the cave. Single file, each man in the tracks of the man in front of him they went. It was a habit to keep any enemy from knowing exactly how many had passed this way. They all kept aware of any sound around them that could be the wounded cat about to strike.

Before they reached the cave, they stopped for a moment and pulled out pine knot torches they had made to light their way in the dark of the cave, as well as keep track of each other. Those who smoked had a pipe full and those who drank took a nip from their flasks. None of them were looking forward to what they had to do next.

"Shouldn't we take up and hide our traps?" Daniel asked quietly.

"No, leave 'em be. They're marked well enough we know where to retrieve them from, and for now, they may come in handy right where they are!" Samuel told him.

"Good point," Christopher interjected.

"Watch fer tracks comin' or goin' and take yer time," Abe instructed. "If'n the cave *does* go all the way through as Tom suspects, tracks may be what leads us through. We're very close to the peaks here and didja notice? They are high and pointed. It may not be that far to go through if it does."

"There may be more than one way inside, it may be more intricate than we suspect, so keep close together and don't fall behind!" Tom directed. He was the leader after all and had to say something. "Shoulder your rifles for now, they will be near useless in some places, I'm sure. Pistols at the ready."

Long brought up his torch and the others lit theirs from his.

"Abe, you still wanna go first?" Tom asked the Kentuckian.

"Yup," Abe replied. "I got my bow, so I'll just need someone at my back with a torch."

"I have your light," Long Walker spoke up, "I know caves."

"Good." Tom nodded. "Sam, I'd like you to bring up the rear, I know your experience with caves as well."

"Done!" was the Scot's quick reply.

Abe started toward the cave with Long Walker behind, stepping over traps and weaving through the brush that scattered their path. How this cat had not gotten snared by more than one trap, Abe mused to himself, was shocking.

The mouth of the cave soon looked before them. Partially hidden by the twisted cedars and scrub brush that grew this high up, it was merely a vertical crack in the face of the mountain, perhaps five feet wide and ten or eleven feet high. Tom had been sitting in just the right place to spot it the other day as it was well hidden from view, except from straight across the valley. Abe took in a deep breath and let it out slowly before he stepped into the cave. It wasn't long before they were in a world of silence and, except for the torches, absolute darkness.

Chapter 15

When I opened my eyes this time, I had no idea how long I had been asleep.

First I noticed the fire had burned low and there was only a dull orange glow of coals in the dark of the cave. There was a little pile of sticks and wood stacked against the far wall and a faint dull gray glow to my right. The next thing I noticed was that seemingly I was alone. My host was nowhere to be seen.

Fighting the pain of movement I slowly climbed my way up the wall to my feet and, using a stick as a crutch, I hobbled over to the fire and fed a few sticks into it. All of a sudden my head began to swim with dizziness, and I felt nauseous from the exertion. I must have hit my head harder than I first thought.

I stood still, taking a moment to clear my head while the sticks I had put in the fire started to catch on. In the growing firelight, I began to investigate the little cave further. From where I stood, I could see no back wall to the cave, and I assumed that meant it was somewhat deeper into the mountain than I first thought. The bit of dull light that came from the front of the cave now appeared to be sunlight.

Where I stood next to the fire, I saw there was a natural wall in front of the mouth of the cave that nearly covered the entrance completely, leaving only a narrow place for a man to walk through. Leaning heavily on my crutch and limping on my injured leg, I slowly made my way to the gap in the stone to get a look at what was outside. As I stepped through, I saw another smaller chamber of the cave which was flooded with sunlight, filtering through branches and brush that had been placed there to conceal the entrance from the outside.

I turned back into the cave and found one branch that had a good-sized knot on it that had been partially burned and set aside. I placed the torch knot into the fire to light it. When it was ablaze, I limped toward the back of the cave to investigate further in. I intended to see how far back this cave went and what might be hidden there in the darkness.

I raised the torch above my head as far as I could without hurting my ribs but still winced in pain. The small chamber I had been recovering in opened up into a much larger chamber, with an underground lake a few yards away. As I hobbled further into the cave I began to hear a dripping of water, seeping into the cave from above and falling into the small lake that probably covered an acre's worth of the cave floor. Here and there I could see shapes in the flickering of the torch. Upon investigating one closer, I found it was a tarpaulin covering a pile of what I assumed to be supplies.

To my surprise, when I lifted the tarp to look it was covering a pile of bales of beaver furs. Under another tarp, I found a pile of traps, and they looked like mine! The fact that Levi brought me to *this* cave was by no means just convenience. As I lifted the tarp on another pile, I heard the rustling of the brush at the entrance, Levi was coming into the 'living chamber'. I quickly replaced the tarp and made my way back to the fire. As the big man stepped through the 'door' of the cave, I was feeding sticks to the fire.

"Ah, it seems you are feeling-a stronger today!" The priest smiled in the firelight. "Is good! How do-a you feel?"

"Some better, yes, Levi. Still tight in my chest and my legs sore as all hell!"

"'Better some,' he says. Ah yes, not too bad if you are-a up on your-a feet!" Levi pointed out.

"No, not bad," I admitted. "What is this place, Levi?" I asked, trying to sound as casual as possible.

"Why, it is-a my home, my son," the priest responded without hesitation.

"Your home?" I was curious. "How long have you lived here?"

"I found-a this place three-a years ago when the Crow released me from-a captivity."

Three years? I thought, astounded. I hoped my surprise was not evident in the dim light. "Does anyone else know of this place?" I asked out loud, trying again to sound casual and not inquisitorial. I was hoping my voice did not betray me through the pain.

"Not a soul," came the priest's reply. "I know how to-a cover my-a tracks and-a keep my secrets!" The last part of that reply worried me just a bit.

but I went on to ask, "So, where did all the bales of beaver come from?" I was pushing my luck now, but in this instance, I felt I had no choice. Not only that but my curiosity had gotten the better of me.

"Why, they are-a yours, my son," the big man responded as if I should already know.

"*Mine?*" I couldn't hold my surprise this time. "How did you . . ." I broke off mid-sentence as the thought came to me. This man had been shadowing me for far longer than I had thought!

"With-a you no being in any-a shape to gather them for the last few days, I-a decided to help you. I assumed you-a were going to-a return through the lion's den again and-a you may want them. After all, trapping is hard work!"

I did a little mental figuring and realized I had been here longer than I had thought.

Dumbstruck for a moment, I listened to the big man continue, "The Crow and-a Blackfeet both-a want your hair, Seniore. I found it wise to keep you out of-a sight and-a recover your furs myself," he explained. "I am nearly ignored by them-a both nowadays. They have begun to-a call me White Medicine Bear, and for them, that means 'great power'. It keeps me safe in-a my travels-a here."

When the big man paused for a moment, my head began to again swirl with thoughts of who this strange man may actually be. For certain he was no priest. Or at least not anymore.

The big man went on to say, "If they were to-a catch you with them yourself, they would-a no doubt torture you before they take your-a scalp!"

"They may find that hard to do!" I broke in. "I am not easy to kill!"

The so-called priest just nodded for a moment before he added, "And now that they-a know this, they will-a hunt you in greater numbers!"

Levi had gotten up and went through to the entrance chamber of the cave and shortly returned with another bale of furs, which I used to sit on by the fire. Again, the priest went out and came in. This time he dragged a small deer into the cave with him.

"At least we won't starve! I thought.

Chapter 16

The Elders and Chiefs had decided to wait for the return of Two Crows and Grassy Hair, who had been sent to the lower land on a scouting trip, before calling the council together.

There had been more rumors of white men in the lowlands at the adobe lodges. This was the place the Mexican traders had always come to trade with his people. Even rival tribes would follow the rules set by the priests and monks who attended the Mission there. The report of more white people there was very concerning to White Eyes and Walks With Ghosts, the chief medicine man in the village. Two Crows and his friend Grassy Hair had volunteered to go see with their own eyes what was happening.

It had been three days since Black Coyote had returned from hunting the trespassing trapper and made his report to White Eyes. He was growing impatient waiting like this while others made up their minds for him about what he must do! He *knew* what must be done. It was how it had always been. They must hunt down this interloper and thief and end his life.

They could not afford to become weak!

These forest and streams had always been here for *his* people and they defended them with ferocity and finality! White Eyes was a wise old man, this was true, but in recent years Black Coyote's opinion was that his wisdom was fading. The whiter the old man's eyes got, the more he began to think like a woman. Didn't he still see the need for vengeance? For justice? The more Black Coyote thought about it, the angrier he got.

He suddenly jumped up from his fire, startling Fox Flower, and stormed out of the tipi into the bright morning sunlight. He paused for a moment to let his eyes adjust from the dim light of the lodge before quickly scanning the camp. There was no smoke coming from the council lodge yet, so he looked to White Eyes' lodge and, as usual, saw the old man sitting outside by his cooking fire. It was a crisp morning and Black Coyote could see the Elder's breath mixing with the smoke of the fire.

He then looked to the lodge of Walks With Ghosts. There was a cloud of thick white smoke coming from the smoke flaps, which usually meant the medicine man was trying to induce a vision. The rest of the camp was in full activity.

The horse boys were out in the hills with the pony herd. The hills were dotted with the 200 or so horses in the herd. The hearty mustango were peacefully grazing the tall valley grasses, some nursing their foals, while the stallion and his segundos kept watch as well. It was how it has always been since the Spaniards had left their horses to them as a gift when they went back to their *own* lands.

Across the camp, he could see the women by the streams where they washed their hair and bathed their babies, filled water skins for the day, and socialized amongst themselves. In the village, people were coming and going, some cooking on their fires, others painting or making their music. Some of the women were scraping buffalo hides from the last great hunt.

The camp was spread far up and down the little valley tucked in the shadows of the mountains. Smoke hung as a haze throughout the camp from the cookfires, and Black Coyote could smell meat cooking.

Everything was as it should be.

But it was not! He looked to the lodges of his two fallen friends and saw no smoke. Their women were in mourning with their families and the lodges were cold. Everything was not as it should be. Another flash of anger went through him, and he began to quickly walk to the lodge of White Eyes. The old man must be made to come to reason!

When he was within earshot he spoke, "White eyes, I must speak with you."

"The morning is bright and warm. Come, sit," the Old One replied. "Tell me your thoughts. I hear in your voice you are angry. As I would be as well."

Black Coyote sat, and for a few moments was silent while he ordered his mind.

He looked at the Great Chief with respect and did not want to let his anger disrespect him. White Eyes just sat with his face turned to the sun feeling its warmth. Even though old age had withered him he was still a large man. He had the frame of a warrior, even now. His hair, once jet black, was now white as the snow. His face though scarred and wrinkled, had a look of understanding and wisdom. He pulled his buffalo robe closer, painted with the sacred symbols of his people as well as his station as a warrior, around his shoulders while he waited for Black Coyote to speak. "Old One," he began, "I must be allowed vengeance. Dull Knife and Running Elk were my brothers. They are now gone, and their killer goes free!" He paused a moment to quiet his voice, "And now, this one is free to steal from us again, and to bring others here! We both know the white men are only thieves, liars, and murderers. They must be taught to respect the Crow people and our home!"

White Eyes held up one hand and spoke quietly, "You have your right to vengeance. It is our way. But you yourself said this one white was different. Did he not merely use trickery to escape when others would have killed? Are not our brothers, Young Bear and Grey Bird, still alive? If it had been the Blackfeet or the Spanish, they would be dead." Black Coyote was quiet and listened carefully to the Old One's words. He was an Old One for a reason. "Did you also tell me when he was captured, he had the opportunity to take scalps and did not? Any other white would take scalps to sell to their Chiefs."

Black Coyote knew this was true as well and nodded. "All this is true," he conceded. "But it is also true that he *did* kill Running Elk and Dull Knife! He was trapping our lands without permission or paying trade. He did not come to us as a friend but as a thief! Only interested in what he could steal!"

The Old One nodded. "This is all true," he admitted. "Perhaps in running him off, you have made him afraid to come again. Perhaps he will stay away. Perhaps you taught him to fear the Crow people."

"I believe he will return," Black Coyote answered. "Whites have no intelligence and no mind for anything but greed. They come and take without asking, and do not learn from the ones who came and died before them."

"It is as you say," the old man nodded as he spoke. "I also remember the words of White Medicine Bear—"

Black Coyote could not help but let a scoff escape his lips.

"—And I have faith in his words. If the Crow people are going to survive, we must look to the coming of a new age. We must adapt to the changing of the seasons."

Black Coyote could only sit with his mouth hanging open. He could not believe his ears! The old man had finally lost his mind!

"We will see what Two Crows and Grassy Hair have to say when they return," the Old One added. "That is all I have to say now."

Black Coyote knew there would be no more debating the Elder at the moment; he would have to wait to say his piece in the council.

The two men sat in silence for quite a while after that, each thinking his thoughts. Black Coyote sat trying to think of ways to not admit he was thinking of his vision. Maybe that was to become true. He had hoped it was just a nightmare brought about by bad food. His pride would not allow him to think any way other than he always had. He was a Warrior! He knew what he was supposed to do, even if the old man did not!

He must protect his people and their way of life even if it meant he lost his own life while doing it! He would not become a dog to the white man like some of the eastern tribes. Look what that got *them*! Some had moved into their summer country and had told them of the decline of their people and the loss of their ancestral lands. Black Coyote would *not* allow that to happen here!

The Warrior and the Elder both sat listening to the sounds of their people around them. Each thought of the best for their people. Each thought to protect the people as best as possible for what was coming into their lives. To preserve their people, their customs and traditions, their stories, and their history. They could just not agree on how *best* to do that. An age-old argument with a new adversary.

An adversary neither of them fully understood.

Chapter 17

The air in the cave was close and dank. Lit by only torches, it was a scene not unlike the stories told of journeys to the center of the Earth. The flames painted eerie scenes on the walls, ranging from the jagged teeth of the mountain to momentary flickers of the faces of demons.

The walls of the cave entrance opened up into a wide chamber, littered with the bones of small animals. In places, it narrowed down again to a space only one man could squeeze through at a time, sometimes only at a crawl. Each man kept his fears to himself as they all fully expected each twist and turn to put them face to face with a very angry lion. Every so often, Abe would stop and strain his ears for any sound of the cat. Not one of the men dared so much as to even breathe hard, for fear of alerting the cat to their presence.

After an hour or so, they came to what seemed to be a fork in their path. They were going to have to make a choice. Left or right. Each tunnel looked as though it could be going in the same direction from this point. Abe thrust his torch into each passage and saw no difference in the flicker of the flame. Behind him, Samuel, David, and Saul were taking advantage of the pause to light new torches as a couple had begun to die out.

It was only then that Abe risked a whisper, "Well, boys, it's anyone's guess which way we should go, so I suppose we ought ta put it to a vote."

"Won't be long and it won't matter!" Tom pointed out. "But I say right."

The others either nodded their agreement or whispered their vote and 'right' was the popular choice.

Abe turned to the right passage and had taken no more than a few steps when they all heard the rattle of a chain in the darkness. Instantly, they all froze in their steps and stopped breathing for a split second. It could be nothing else but the sound of the chain the lion had dragged off when it ensnared itself and got away with the trap still on its paw. The next thing they all heard was the low growl of a mountain lion.

It seemed to be coming from *behind them*!

Now a cave has a funny way of making sound travel. It could bounce off walls at weird angles, bending the sound, and making it hard to tell exactly where it was coming from.

"Now what?" A whisper came in the silence. It was Chris McNeil.

As one mind, they all cocked their pistols or drew their weapons and strained their eyes and ears into the darkness.

"Back to back, boys!" Abe said loudly, knowing there was no more use for stealth. "It'll be tight but—"

He was cut off sharply by the scream of a mountain cat as the lion leaped upon them from the darkness.

Abe roared in pain as he was the first to be attacked by the wounded cat. He tried a shot with his pistol but it went wide, hitting the cave wall. The cat's jaws clamped shut on Abe's neck and they all heard a sickening crunch. Abe's body slumped to the floor of the cave and the cat shook him violently to make sure he was dead. Three pistols fired at the cat and the beast dropped Abe's body and turned, screaming at the pack of humans invading its home.

The cat leaped again, this time toward Saul as he was trying to reload his pistol for another shot. Cole jumped between him and the cat and fired a shot, but he caught the full force of the cat's assault, and his shot went wild, careening down the passageway. The raging lion snapped at Cole's neck but Cole was able to shove his pistol into the lion's mouth, thus saving himself for the moment.

All torches had by now been abandoned to the floor as every man in the cave converged on the cat. Samuel had his tomahawk and knife at the ready, but the McNeil brothers were between him and the lion and were scrambling to position themselves to strike. Saul had finished reloading his pistol and was lining up for a shot—literally in the dark—when the cat twisted and thrashed and suddenly, Cole was in the line of fire.

Tom had worked his way up one wall of the passage and now buried his tomahawk into the cat's flank, causing the cat to drop Cole and roar in pained rage. It snapped its jaws at Tom, but he was no longer there. Chris tried for a stab at the throat of the thrashing cat and missed. The cat retaliated and slashed at Chris's belly, ripping him open with one swipe.

David roared like a beast himself, "NOOOOOO!" He leaped onto the back of the twisting animal. Cole slipped and went down, so Saul took his shot and the ball tore a hole in the cat's shoulder while at the same time, Cole thrust upward with his knife. David hacked down on the shoulders of the cat with his camp ax.

Samuel got a clear shot and put a pistol ball into the side of the writhing and now furious lion. The cat clamped down on Chris' throat to finish him off and soon every man was on top of the beast, stabbing and hacking at it in a frenzy. Tom had taken up the chain to the trap on the cat's paw, in order not only to pull it off the now dying man but to distract it and draw it away. The big lion gave one more thrust at Cole who was lying partly under Chris' body and partially under the cat itself.

"Git it offa me! Git it offa me!" he screamed.

Long Walker came in with his tomahawk and buried it into the skull of the huge beast and it dropped like a stone.

"Git it offa me!" Cole yelled again.

David began stabbing the beast over and over again, screaming a primal sound that scared everyone else even more than the cat had!

"Get them torches before they go out!" Tom shouted. Long and Samuel had already taken up one each and held them high as they could for the light. The scene was one of complete carnage!

Chris McNeil had been torn nearly in two by the talons of the lion and his throat was gone. Abraham was lying in a heap against one wall of the passage bleeding out through holes in his throat and eye, his other staring lifelessly into the darkness.

Everywhere was the sickly sweet, coppery smell of blood mixed with the acrid scent of gun smoke. David knelt at his brother's side, openly weeping while stroking his brother's long red hair out of his eyes to close them. Long Walker handed Tom one of the torches and Samuel began reloading his pistol.

"Tom, we better git reloaded and skedaddle outta here before we lose the rest of our light, we ain't got too many torches left."

"I agree," Tom said simply and began reloading his pistol with shaky hands.

Cole reverently relieved Abe of his weapons, as they were useless to him now, and may come in handy later on. David did not move from his brother's side.

The others followed Long down the passageway and Tom said quietly, "David . . ."

Samuel held up his hand to silence him and Tom heard David praying over his brother between sobs.

"Sam!" Tom asserted. "We gotta go!"

Samuel just nodded and said, "Shhh."

David finished his prayer and he and Samuel made the sign of the cross. David leaned down and kissed his brother's head and stood simply saying "I'll be takin' him back home in the spring." He followed Samuel and Tom. One by one, they turned their thoughts from their companions, now lying dead in the cave, to the task at hand, which was getting out of this cave.

It wasn't long before the remaining torches burned out one by one and the men were left in complete darkness to continue, feeling their way like blind men in the utter blackness. For an eternity they inched forward, some using their flint and steel to catch glimpses of their path in the short flashes of the sparks.

After what seemed like an entire day of this, the men finally felt their way out into the open air again! They had found the eastern entrance to the cave! For a moment, all their fear and sense of loss subsided as they realized Tom was right! They had found a shortcut to the eastern side of the mountain range!!

The elation soon subsided, as they began taking stock of their wounds and supplies. They were covered, to a man, with splatters of blood. They stood for just a moment taking in the lung-fulls of the crisp, fresh air and calming their hearts which were still beating nearly out of their chests.

They had taken a gamble and it had proven costly indeed! They had lost two men and three more were injured. David was limping from a badly twisted knee and had a bite on his arm that was still dripping blood. Saul had a serious gash on his right thigh and found his blood was what was making his steps in his moccasins slippery. Tom had a gunshot wound in the meaty part of his shoulder, that from the looks of it, was certainly a ricochet. It had missed the bone, which was certainly lucky for him, though he didn't feel lucky at the time. The party was going to have to keep moving. They had little water and they were going to need to clean and bind their wounds before they became infected. Infection was the number one killer in situations like this. The bite of a cat was certain to cause it, not to mention the claws.

Indeed, it had been a costly gamble! But aside from the shock of the battle and the losses of their compadres, they all knew one thing. They had found Silas' secret passage! His closely guarded secret!

Now they just needed to find Silas!

Chapter 18

Two Crows and Grassy Hair hid their horses among a stand of trees on a little hillside above the adobe lodges.

From here they would go on foot.

The 'adobe lodges' was a gathering of ramshackle buildings surrounding the old Spanish mission that stood there for ages. Now, even though the Mission was still in use, the little village was a crossroads trading post on what was becoming known as the Santa Fe Trail.

In addition to the small Mission, there was a trading post, corrals and barn for horses, a boarding house of sorts, and several small huts and houses where permanent residents lived. On any other day, one may have looked at the town and thought it was abandoned. Normally the stockyard and pens were empty, and the buildings' shutters were all closed against the high desert winds.

Today though, there were wagons on the outskirts of the little town, and the blacksmith shop at the barn was billowing smoke and one could hear the rhythmic *ta-tink ta-tink ta-tink* of the blacksmith at work. There was a group of people gathered, weeping over a freshly dug grave as a priest said a prayer, in the small cemetery plot just west of the town. The corral and stockyard pens were filled with horses and cattle, and there was a general commotion of activity that gave the all the impressions of a thriving community.

In the distance to the east, Grassy Hair pointed out to his companion a dust cloud that could only be more white men, in their wagons with their cows, coming into their lands. Walks With Ghosts was right. The medicine man had told of a vision of countless white people coming from across the prairie and consuming the land of the Crow and their rivals the Blackfeet, the Ute, Navajo, Apache, and all the tribes.

They had heard the stories of how the whites had come from across the big water and spread over the lands to the east, even so far as the lands of the Kiowa and Comanche to the south. Now it seemed they would never stop coming. Were Walks With Ghosts' visions to come true? As far as Two Crows and Grassy Hair could see, the answer was plain. They were certainly going to have to fight to keep their lands from being overrun by the whites.

White Eyes had charged them with gathering information, but neither could believe even *he* could have foreseen this! It seemed the almost deserted little pueblo had sprouted new life! As indeed it had. And with this new life came a whole new problem for the Crow people and all the tribes. Neither Two Crows nor Grassy Hair would admit it, but they were suddenly afraid, and neither of them wanted to give this news to White Eyes and the Council.

Slowly, the pair retreated down the hill to where their horses were tied and mounted up for the ride back to the village in the hills.

Chapter 19

I couldn't put my finger on it but something was off.

I just couldn't overcome the feeling that there was more to what was going on than I was being told. I didn't necessarily think Levi was lying to me, but having just met under such odd circumstances, he had good reason to keep his own council; as did I. In truth, I had to admit, it wasn't really any of my business anyway. I had my own plans and they took precedence over anything else at this point.

Still, I had not yet discovered what else was hidden in the rear of the cave. I had briefly seen several piles covered with tarps and had assumed it was all my furs as Levi had said. Things were adding up wrong though. I was suspicious, though I had nothing clear to tell me there was any weight behind my suspicion. Now that I was stronger and the pain had mostly subsided, I decided I needed a better look at the rear chamber and its contents.

No matter how much I still hurt, I was going to have to get to the cave and just hope that this time, like the time before, I could make it through when the lion was out hunting. I would have to be extremely cautious.

I stood leaning against the wall in the entrance of Levi's cave, looking out east over the valley below. The weather was shaping up to storm again and I could smell snow in the air. I couldn't risk staying to rehabilitate any longer, I would have to go soon, or the way would be blocked for sure!

It had been nearly two weeks now I had been recovering in Levi's cave. Levi would come and go as mysteriously as his presence in these mountains was in the first place. Now and then he would come back to the cave with bales of furs on his back, other times with game to cook or wood for the fire.

The valley below had been covered now with a blanket of snow, while on the mountainside the winds had caused drifts in the low areas.

Around the cave, there was only a dusting of snow. Even though it was snowing now, it didn't seem enough to prevent me from making my trip back to the camp on the other side of the mountains. I would have to leave the bulk of the furs I collected until I could return next season. I did not want to reveal any caches of furs to Levi that he had not already found. They would be safe where they were hidden.

Levi's trips away now only produced game or wood for the fire and were less frequent as the air became biting cold most days. On days like today, we talked. In any other setting, we might have discussed current events whether at home or abroad, but that was for men of society and there was no society here. We talked of philosophy and religion, or the layout and detail of the valley below; the latter being Levi's favorite subject.

"I believe you are-a lucky this year! The Indians call this the wet mountain valley for a reason. Usually there is-a more snow by this time of the year," Levi explained. I only half listened anymore, as usually, Levi repeated things he had already said, as men who have lived alone have a proclivity to do. "There is much snow to deal with, yes, but it is not impossible to traverse by foot until ya reach higher places. It is the ice that will kill ya as you well know!" Levi said.

The big man chuckled to himself while he poked the low glowing fire. When he put the last few pieces of wood on it, I knew I would get the opportunity I needed. Levi's trips for wood were getting longer as he had to go further to procure it. I knew I would have nearly an hour to explore further into the rear chamber of the cave.

"When I return," Levi said as he tied his rope belt around his big bearskin coat, "there is something I must discuss with you before you go. I see you are strong enough to make the trip. I assume you wish to go soon, no?"

"I notice, Levi, that your English has improved with my tutoring you." I smiled. "Whatever will you do without me?"

Levi just smiled through his broken teeth, pulled the bear head hood over his head, and simply said, "What I have always done." He then left for his wood-gathering excursion.

I waited for about ten minutes before getting up and putting a torch I'd made, from pieces of my torn clothing and fatwood from the firewood Levi gathered, into the fire to light. This would burn much brighter and longer than a pine knot torch and would give me plenty of time to explore. I had only a slight limp to my step now as I made my way through the narrow passage at the rear of the cave into the cavern beyond.

The familiar *drip, drip, drip,* came to my ears as I came near to the opening. The first thing I noticed was this cavern was much larger than I originally thought, extending for hundreds of feet in all directions from the opening. The next thing I noticed was that there were also more tarp-covered piles. I knew the ones close to the entrance that I had investigated before were furs. But now I could see many more hidden behind a curve in the wall face, in the formerly dimly lit reaches of the cave.

As I wandered around and lifted one of the tarps, I found bits and pieces of Spanish uniforms and weapons. Under another, I found surveying equipment, a broken compass, a sextant, and charts; some only half drawn. I couldn't understand the language the maps were written in but I knew it had to be Spanish. Something was familiar about the way the maps were drawn. They were drawn by someone who knew nautical terms, as there were notes that looked to be some sort of coordinates in certain places. Marking what, I didn't know, but they looked similar to those I had seen years and years ago on the ship. I shuddered a bit at this thought but blamed it on the chill in the air.

Then it caught my eye, a term even I knew. Sangre De Cristo, 'Blood of Christ', written over the face of a range of mountains that extended down as far as the deserts in Mexico. This particular map was drawn in great detail and even included notes that seemed to be the names of the tribes that frequented the surrounding regions. Instantly, I knew the worth of this and quickly and carefully rolled it up. I replaced everything else as it was before replacing the tarp.

This *one* piece of parchment was going to be worth more than even all the beaver I had collected, perhaps worth more than all the hides and furs my company had collected as well! I quickly looked around to make sure I left no sign I had been there and returned through the passage.

As I had calculated, I had plenty of time to secure the map in my pack and burn my torch in the fire, so that when Levi returned carrying the now routine-looking bundle of dead limbs in on his back, I was seated back on my bale of beaver skins warming my hands by the fire.

The rest of the afternoon we sat discussing the contours of the valley and the conditions on the trail that would lead me back to the tunnel cave.

"I will be leaving in the morning," I said abruptly. "If this threat of snow holds off, that is. I've got people who will be very worried by now that I have not returned."

Levi nodded but sat in silence, cutting some meat up into a pot to make a broth.

"You said you had something you wanted to tell me before I left?" I prodded him a bit.

Finally, after some silence, Levi replied, "You must keep me and my presence here a secret, no one can know. I fear for my safety with the Indians if it is known that I have any involvement with their enemies. And they see you as their enemy. Perhaps this will change in the future, but who knows the future?"

"I can give you my word that anyone I could tell would not believe me, let alone give any weight to the story. But I will agree, on one condition."

Levi looked me in the eye for a very rare occasion and asked, "And that would be?"

I took a moment before starting, unsure if I should go on, choosing my words carefully. "I want to return and trap here next season, I have seen the richness of this territory and I want you to negotiate with the Indians for me. I want them to understand I want to trade with them. I can bring goods, the like of which they cannot imagine, in trade for the furs."

I paused a moment while Levi nodded and looked back to his cooking on the fire.

"You hold some sway with these Indians here. I think if we partner up we can do well together. And I'll warrant that would keep us both holding each other's secret now, wouldn't it?"

"That will not be an easy task," Levi replied simply. "I will think on it and answer before you leave."

I did not want to press the issue and let it drop for the time being. I knew a priest had no need for prosperity or earthly riches, so the fact this man Levi would consider it, coupled with his request to be kept a secret, threw doubt into my mind that Levi was the man he said he was.

After some more discussion, Levi handed me a gourd bowl of stew. While I blew on it to cool it, Levi made his request again, "You will consider what we talked about here? I believe in the end it will benefit you as well." I put the stew to my lips to test if it was cool enough and Levi went on. "I will help you, But I must be helped in return."

"And how could I help *you*?" I was curious. "You understand *my own* business must come first, and I have partners with whom I must discuss anything first."

Levi nodded at this and met my gaze, "I will help you with your business on one condition," he said. "You will help me by showing the Crow, Blackfeet, Cheyenne, and other tribes that not *all* whites are thieves and liars as they believe." I could only sit and eat while Levi went on, "I believe there is room for all to live in peace with each other, but you must not come here to conquer like the Spanish but to offer brotherhood to the Tribes. Believe me, they know how to make war, and they will if you come here to take without giving them the opportunity to know you as a friend."

"I certainly have no intentions of making war with anyone, I spent my days at war in my youth and I grew tired of it even then," I responded. I didn't fully believe the so-called priest, but in my current position I could only tentatively agree, so leaving my answer ambiguous seemed the prudent choice.

"I know you will do the right thing," Levi said, effectively ending the conversation.

The rest of the day was spent getting me and my gear ready for my trip back to the western faces of the range, packing food for a few days, and binding my ribs and sore knee for better use while on the journey.

The next morning, I awoke to Levi fashioning a cane made from an Aspen sapling. Aspen have a root that grows at a ninety degree angle from the trunk of the tree, which made a good handle to lean on, better than the straight stick I had been using.

He offered to show me back to where I had fallen and see me on my way, though I didn't feel I needed a guide I agreed out of appreciation for what the priest had done for me these last couple of weeks. Surely if Levi had not been present, I would have died, trapped in a ravine and frozen.

There was a light snow falling, but the temperature was balmy for a winter day, making the going somewhat easy. I was glad I had not waited any longer before leaving, as it looked to be shaping up for a big storm. It took nearly an hour to reach the spot where I had fallen into the ravine and injured myself. I was amazed the old priest had been able to extract me in the first place, let alone carry me for an hour through the wilderness to his little cave hideout.

When we reached the spot Levi simply said, "Good luck my son," and turned to leave.

"I owe you my thanks, Levi," I offered as the big man walked away, but he just waved a hand over his shoulder as if to dismiss it.

It took me nearly the rest of the day to reach the mouth of the tunnel cave where I found, to my surprise, the tracks of several men leading from it. The tracks were not very old, as today's snow had not completely filled them yet. Upon closer inspection, I found blood splatters and a couple of knot torches. I also noticed these were not the tracks of any local tribes, but the tracks of white men! Tom's tracks I readily recognized; he had bigger feet than most men. Which meant Tom had come to find him and had brought help!

Most of the tracks led away from the cave mouth and were quickly disappearing in the newly falling snow, but two sets of tracks led back into the cave, along with a blood trail. I fashioned a new torch from one of the burnt-out ones there, wrapping it in wool strips from an old blanket and some pine tar I carried in my tinder box for just such a need. With a little dry grass and cedar bark, I soon had a small fire going. While I gathered up my courage to enter the cave, I warmed up some meat to eat.

Suppose I'll just have to chance it, I thought to myself. *Whoever went back through was injured and may run into the mountain lion.*

I slowly ate my small meal and watched the cave mouth intently as if I could summon the cat to exit by sheer will, so I could go through back to the other side in safety. After eating, I tied Long Stick to my pack as it was useless in the closeness of the cave.

With a sigh, I said aloud, "Well, can't avoid it any longer."

I lit my torch in the fire before kicking snow over it and entering the cave with the hint of a prayer on my mind. Wishing I still had powder for my pistol, I drew my tomahawk with one hand and held the torch aloft with the other. With a feeling of renewed determination, I walked into the darkness. I did not relish running into a mountain lion in my injured condition but I had no choice at this point.

The tracks faded as the floor of the cave was without snow, but the blood trail continued. Sometimes the drops were close together and sometimes spaced far apart, leading me to believe whoever was bleeding was starting to get it stopped by this point. Soon, I came to a narrow place where there were *pools* of blood on the floor. It was still somewhat sticky and not completely dried yet, meaning whatever had happened here had been quite recent. From the amount of blood, some great battle had happened here.

I told myself I needed to keep moving, as the cat who lived here may be getting near. Instead, I took the time and looked closer at the tracks. In one spot I found tufts of golden hairs stuck in the drying blood.

The cat!

My mind began to piece together what had happened and I physically sighed with relief. Maybe the lion was dead! If so, someone had paid a dear price for it, for near as I could tell, three bodies had bled out here.

When I finally pulled myself away from the scene of all that carnage and death, I tried to pick up the pace. Unfortunately, my stiff leg still hampered my progress despite the cane Levi had made me.

For the rest of the trip through the cave, I thought of what had led to this point, mistakes I may have made, and Levi's proposition. What should I do when the time came? In my hampered condition, it took me most of the night, along with several rest periods, to reach the other end of the cave.

When I did at last step out of the cave, I had another surprise waiting for me.

Chapter 20

The trip through the cave had taken more time than I thought. When I stepped out of the cave it was into the sunlight. Though this side of the mountains was in the morning shadow of the peaks, it was very bright compared to the black of the cave.

I stood, blinking for a moment to focus my eyes. When I could see well enough to walk again, I took no more than a few steps out of the cave and around the scrub oaks and twisted hemlocks at the mouth, when I saw two stone-covered graves. Next, I saw the carcass of a lion hanging from a limb of a nearby spruce. David McNeil was skinning the beast while Saul was attending to a small fire.

"Don't forget to save the skull!" I shouted.

Both men turned with a start like they had heard a gunshot!

"I don't think Tom has a mountain cat yet!" I added.

Saul, always quick of wit, just smiled and yelled back, "Well *this* one's got a hole in it!"

When I was seated by the fire, Saul asked, "Where the *hell* you *been*, man? We thought you was dead! Tom's been worried sick, not to mention the rest of us!!"

"Worried, huh? *Tom*?"

Saul went on, "Yeah, worried you wasn't gonna make it to rendezvous and make us all that money you promised!"

I could only chuckle slightly as laughter hurt my ribs. "Well, *that* sounds more likely!"

"Good ta see yous in one piece, old man!" David chimed in, still skinning the cat. "I hope your trip was worth it! My brother's *dead* 'cause of—"

"DAVID!" Saul cut him off short. "That's enough, what's happened is done, and it weren't Silas' fault!"

David only turned back to the cat with a "Pfft!"

"So, one was Christopher, who is the other'n buried there?" I asked.

"Abe Hatfield," Saul replied. "He was the one who took the lead through the cave to find you. He was a brave man, certainly braver than me!" he admitted.

"Like yous care," David said under his breath.

I just looked at him for a moment, then continued the conversation. "Both were good men," I said solemnly. "I'm sorry you lost Chris this way, David. I truly am."

To which David again just loosed another "Pffft!" and refused to even look at me

"This way of life has its taxes, too!" I went on, knowing David's thoughts on taxes of any kind. "And it collects at the most inconvenient times!"

"*Inconvenient?*" David spat, "Inconvenient to who? I *hope* you mean to his family and kin! And to *me*! As him was me right hand and a better man than you! Not to *you* and yer quest for furs and fortune, Silas Horn!"

I understood the young man's ire at the loss of his brother, as I too had lost a brother in the past, but that was another life. "Yes, that is what I mean." I nodded. "But also inconvenient to us all! We will miss him, he was well-liked by the crew, as you know. Of course, your brother's share will go to you now, David, as I know you'll be wantin' it to send to your kin."

The look on David's face belied he didn't feel this was enough of an apology but he only stated, "I'll be takin' his bones *and* his share come spring!" He then leaned over the fire and looked me directly in the eye, his face smeared with the cat's blood still, "And I'll not be lookin' back! I done had enough of these mountains, these savages, and *you*, Silas!" He turned back to skinning the cat and went on half under his breath, "I've had enough I 'ave. . cold nights, freezing me bones, no hearth to warm at night, no woman; nothing but the threat of death all round us!"

I let him talk and rested in the sun for a bit, as it was just peeking over the ridge above. While the other two finished the cat and began cutting meat from its bones.

"Where are the others?" I asked Saul, half knowing the answer already.

"They went lookin' for *you*, they did!" David answered. "Which, I *suppose*, means *now* we're gonna have to go on through that wretched hole again and go lookin' fer them, too!"

"You have grieving to do, David," I told him. "Saul and I will find the others. Looks like you got healin' to do, too!" I pointed out he was bleeding from a bandage on his forearm.

"*Damn* it all!" David spat and tied the knot on his bandage tighter.

It looked like snow, so we decided to camp in the mouth of the cave, after much argument from David who wanted nothing to do with "That damn hole!"

While we ate, we made plans to go and find Tom and the others. David would stay behind and gather up the horses from down below in the valley, while Saul and I would go find Tom.

Saul and I talked deep into the night over the fire. I told him of my flight from the Crow, and of Levi. I didn't feel it was prudent to share my discovery of the map just yet, that could wait for another day.

After David drifted off in his blankets and after much thought, I decided that when we found Tom, weather permitting, we would go for the bales of fur in Levi's cave. Hopefully, Levi would be gone and I could get a longer look at the stores in the rear chamber of the cave.

When Saul too was asleep, I thought of Paul and his crew, who had gone to the north of the Low Pass when I came south with Tom and his crew. How had they fared? Had they been fortunate? Or had some Blackfeet or Crow lifted their hair? It was one thing to be a member of such a venture as this, but it was completely different being the leader.

There was much more responsibility to being the leader. More worry, sleeplessness, and stress as well. I knew about responsibility from my time in the Navy after the turn of the century, but now I was dealing with the practical applications of that responsibility in a completely different way. And in a completely hostile land!

These two men had lost their lives because of a venture I led them on! Because of *my* decisions, two good men had given their life's blood for me. It was something that weighed heavily on my mind. Sleep did not come easy this night, nor for many nights to come.

When sleep did come, I was again assaulted by my dreams.

The woman with the soulful haunting eyes and beautiful smile. As always, she spoke but no sound came to my ears. She touched me but I felt nothing. She was trying to tell me something, but I could not understand. Her deep blue eyes were both frightened and sad, her features framed by long, wavy, almost wild chestnut hair, tinged with red when the sun shone through it. She turned her head to speak to someone behind her, and when she turned back there was only fear in her eyes!

I could see her lips form the words, "HELP ME!" Though no sound came.

She touched my face gently and instantly I was awake. She was gone. Who was this woman who haunts my dreams? What danger was she in that she begged for my help? No answers came to mind, and I lay once more to sleep.

Only this time there were no dreams.

Chapter 21

The next morning there was four new inches of snow on the mountains and a dusting in the valley below. David left early to go round up the horses while Saul and I made our way back through the cave to the east side of the mountains. I would go to Levis cave and Saul would try to track down the rest of the crew.

Now that the cat was dead, and they had been through this passage before the going seemed much easier and soon they stepped out into the light of the eastern side of the cave. With words of good luck, Saul split off to go down below and find the crew while I made my way to Levis cave, watching for tracks along the way.

As I approached the cave I saw no tracks, no sign anyone was near. I dropped my pack on what Levi called the "doorstep" of the cave and hollered into it. "Levi!? Anyone to home?!"

There came no answer so I assumed the big man was gone. After I got a fire going, I went to have a better look in the rear chamber of the cave.

I took a torch and an armload of wood into the rear chamber and started a fire there so I could see better than just by torchlight. Once it was going brightly, I turned my attention to the piles of supplies I had seen before. Upon closer inspection, there were more documents and papers that were in Spanish, as well as old, rusted muskets, and powder in wooden casks. In one pile there were spades and picks for mining or tunneling. Beside one of the tarped piles, I found wooden crates. They were tightly nailed shut, but with my knife, I was able to open one. It was full of rocks. I opened another. The same.

I closed them back up and decided to explore further toward the back of the cave. I took the torch from the fire and skirted the little lake and went looking for the back wall of the cave.

Levi had insisted there was no end to this cave that he had found but I wanted to see for myself.

Something was not right about all this, and I needed to know what it was.

On the other side of the lake, the walls closed down to a passageway of sorts. It became quite narrow and I had to walk sideways to fit through some places. The ceiling began to close down on me as well. In places, I had to crouch to avoid hitting my head. In others, I had to step around the cone shapes protruding up from the floor wherever there was a drip of water. Just as I thought about turning back, the wall opened just a bit to a small chamber about the size of the entryway. This was very clearly the end of the cave as there was no other passage leading out.

On the floor, a little to one side of the entrance, there lay a skeleton in burlap wrapping that had rotted away long ago. Beside the bones was a Latin Bible, and a pair of rope sandals. I took up the Bible and decided, as my torch was burning low, that I had seen enough now to tell me Levi was *not* what he said he was at all! I remembered that Levi had said this was a cache left from the Spanish conquests of this land. But many of the things I had just seen were too modern to be leftover from the Spanish.

Some piece of the puzzle was still missing.

I returned to the front chambers and started taking my bales out to the doorstep chamber, trying to figure out what I had just learned, and how Levi fitted into it. Once I had all my bales stacked at the ready out front, I felt hunger pangs and realized I had not eaten any breakfast. I sat on a bale and pulled some jerky from my pack to chew on.

There was certainly more going on than met the eye here. Who was the man in the rear of the cave? What would a 'priest' need with mining tools and surveying equipment? There would be time to think on these things after I accomplished my more important goal here. That goal was to collect my furs and get them and my men back to the other side of the mountain, and thus back to relative safety for the winter.

Saul had gone no more than a couple miles from the cave mouth before he spotted a trail in the snow that could be no one else but Tom and the men.

Taking advantage of the moment for a breather, he took out his spyglass and searched the trail down into the valley. To his surprise, it looked as if the men had been joined by another from the north. Or at least, there was a single trail coming down from north of where he was which merged with the trail of the men he was following.

Looking over the valley for a sign, he took in the sun peeking through the mists on the hilltops to the east. The light gave the valley floor a mystical and eerie look on days like this, like peering into a dream. As he studied the terrain through his glass, it looked as if there was a hint of smoke behind a low hill a mile or so down the mountain. Was it smoke? Was it just thicker fog? He decided it was worth a look since that was the way the trail went anyway.

As Saul walked, ever the true mountain man that he was, he used all his senses to take in every nuance of his surroundings. The caw of a crow in the distance warned his mate there was a human nearby. The smell of a crisp, cold, mountain morning filled his lungs with good clean air.

He saw the shades of blue through the fog, evidence that were the low hills and buttes across the valley floor. To the south, a coyote stood in his tracks watching the man pass with an almost certain enmity for humans. If Saul had not been on the rescue mission he was on, he may have enjoyed this adventure into an unknown land.

Soon he smelled smoke as he neared the hillside he had seen through his glass. He took a moment to check his weapons for readiness just in case this was *not* whom he was looking for. As he started forward again, he slowed his pace so he wouldn't be too loud crunching through the icy snow.

When he heard familiar voices, he shouted, "HELLO THE CAMP! DON'T SHOOT NOW!"

The answer came back, "Come on in, Saul! And meet a new friend!" Tom answered.

Then Cole shouted also, "Took ya long enough! Long done seen ya a mile back!"

"I was waitin' fer ya ta get eyes on me so's I din't get shot!" Saul countered with a smile. "I know some of ya are a little quick on the trigger!"

When Saul walked into the little camp, he set his eyes on the biggest man he had ever seen! Even without the bearskin coat and hood, he stood head and shoulders above everyone else in the camp.

"Saul, this is Father Levi," Tom introduced the large man. "The good padre here tells us Silas was on his way back to the other side yesterday morning. We just missed him after we went through the cave!"

"That's right," Levi offered. "It's a good thing I-a find you and save you the trouble of searching. It would be best for everyone if-a you are back on the other side of the mountain soon!" He went on to explain Silas' caches of furs both in his cave and down in the valley below. "Perhaps it's-a best you leave them for now, and come back in the spring. Perhaps this valley will be a bit more welcoming when you next return."

Saul broke in again, "Look, we better get to movin', if'n we go now, we can still follow the padre's tracks back to the cave where Silas is and at least get the bales we have there."

Tom agreed, "We need to get back before this storm hits bad and we get cut off!"

By the time they reached the cave, I had all the bales out on the front porch and was just about to shoulder one to carry to the lions cave. "Well look who showed up just in time! We got a lot of furs here to move and I been feeling a mite poorly lately!" I said. "Well at least ya had the sense to make half bales so's a man can carry em for once!" Tom said as he smiled and near lifted me off my feet in a bear hug. "I thought we had lost ya brother! I figgered you fer a pile o bones in the woods somewhere by now!"

"All right, all right, Tom, that's enough," I grunted through the wave of pain. "Lemme down, I gotta breathe!"

He pretty much dropped me back on my feet. "I'm so sorry, man. I didn't know ya was hurt bad!"

"I'll be fine in a few days. For now, let's just get these furs where they belong and be done with this place for the winter!"

"All righty, boys! Ya heard the boss man! We got half a winter's work to do yet, let's get on it!" Tom ordered with a huge smile on his face. "And *you*, Silas!" he said to me. "Next time you feel like goin' off galivanting by yerself in new territory yet, yer gonna have to take me with you!"

By nightfall, we, and our bales, were all safely through the cave once again and back on the west face of the range. The next morning, when we were rested and full from a good hot meal, they listened to what had happened while I was away.

"Well, it's good to have you back safe with us again!" Tom mused after I told my story. "And don't ya go off and scare me like that again, ya hear?"

That night, after we sat around the fire, swapping stories and passing the jug of whiskey that was left, I took Tom aside and showed him the map I had found in Levi's cave, and told him the rest of the story, and what I had found there. Tom couldn't read Spanish either but agreed it would be best to keep the existence of the map between us until the season was over, and let the men part ways or choose to sign on for another season. David surely would be one to not trust with this information. So we didn't speak of it again that winter.

My thoughts turned to the work at hand and how to best supply for a whole new venture in the coming season. I thought again of my partner, Paul Mcveigh, and his crew to the north. Did any survive? Long Walker had brought no news from them in a month.

Always one to think positively until proven wrong, Tom insisted they were fine and had probably had just as good a season as we had, "Maybe better considering we got the insane one here!" Tom said sardonically.

"Well, I'm still alive, and I still got all my parts a workin'!" I said to him. "So, let's just do what we can with this year, salvage what we can, and make better plans for next year!"

The rest of the season went pretty smoothly in comparison to the adventure I had been on. I felt lucky to be alive but also felt something in my bones that gave me pause. Nothing solid I could put a finger on, just a feeling that maybe we hadn't seen the last of the danger in this great adventure we were on.

Most of all, I felt the relief and absolute thrill of still being alive after coming so close to death so many times during my scouting trip. I certainly would not make the same mistakes I had made this time.

And now I had an advantage no one else had.

None of my competitors, I would venture to guess, had a map of previously unknown territory to guide them. I would certainly be well prepared for the next step in my plan to explore new territories, see new lands, and maybe find the woman who haunted my dreams.

All my life I had wandered in search of the place that would be home. I had always been one to be perpetually in search of the next best adventure, to aimlessly go from one place to another, never feeling like I fit anywhere. From what I had seen of this new territory over the last few weeks, I now knew where I belonged.

I just had to find the right way to make it happen!

www.ingramcontent.com/pod-product-compliance
Lightning Source LLC
Chambersburg PA
CBHW062233150726
47991CB00006B/2566